The Case of the Intrepid Investigator

A Work of Fiction

by

William Henry Jenkins

The Case of the Intrepid Investigator

The Case of the Intrepid Investigator

Edition 2

Published by William Jenkins

Email: williamhenryjenkins@gmail.com

Telephone: 1-613-217-0940

The author wished to acknowledge the careful proof reading and many corrections submitted by **Dawn Rumble** of Trenton, Canada who tirelessly and gratuitously suggested the improvements.

The Case of the Intrepid Investigator is a work of fiction. Names, characters, places, and incidents are the products of the author's imagination or are used fictitiously. Any resemblance to actual events, locales, businesses, companies, or persons, living or dead, is entirely coincidental.

ISBN Paperback   978-1-928164-75-3

ISBN Electronic   978-1-928164-76-0

The Case of the Intrepid Investigator

The Case of the Intrepid Investigator

For Barbara and Tony Rego,

Celebrating more than fifty years of friendship

The Case of the Intrepid Investigator

The Case of the Intrepid Investigator

Author's Note: In case you happen in error to take this story seriously, I would like you to realize that I'm poking fun at myself and at some of the stuffed shirts I've met in my journey of life. This is truly a work of fiction, brought about by the solitude and isolation caused by the covid-19 pandemic. If you get the odd chuckle out of it, I'll be happy.

Chapter 1

I'm enjoying a quiet coffee in a nearly deserted restaurant in the Bayshore Inn in downtown Linden at about 9 o'clock on a Sunday night. A young lady in her early twenties enters the restaurant and hurries to my booth. She sits opposite me and simply says "Pretend I'm with you."

"I'm Bill," I say, and she replies 'Kate'.

"Would you like a coffee or something to eat?"

"A sandwich and a coffee, please."

I signal the waitress and order a grill cheese sandwich with fries, a coffee with cream and sugar, plus a refill for me. Kate stares straight at me and seems a little relieved behind her face mask. I give her an encouraging smile while wondering why this young lady with her braided hair needs to pretend that she is with me. Her skin is a beautiful brown, showing African ancestry. She has big, inviting, brown eyes and a good figure.

"Is someone looking for you? Someone who knows you?" I ask.

"Yes and no," she replies. "If anyone comes in, don't look at them. Just keep chatting. It'll be O.K."

"I don't think we will fool anyone into thinking we're man and wife," I comment. "You could be my granddaughter."

She removes her mask and smiles.

"What can we chat about?" she asks.

"The American election or covid-19. Take your pick," I say. "I'm glad that Trump didn't win, and Linden has very few covid cases."

"Sorry to spoil your evening," she says. "What are your plans?"

"It's after nine," I reply. "I'm heading for some shuteye when you've finish toying with me."

"I'm not toying with you. I need some help in a hurry and you are the first person I found."

She wears a business suit on a Sunday night, not the sloppy jeans we've grown to expect on the younger generation. I don't think she's a lay minister, though.

"I suppose there's a rather large man who is going to demand that I pay him for your services. I bet he won't even deduct the cost of your snack."

I'm a man of the world. I've been around. I can tell when a lady is a lady of the night. After all, it is night-time. It is pitch dark outside at nine p.m. in November. Of course, I am flattered that this pretty girl even looks at me, but she probably must earn her keep and may figure that even an old goat is better than nothing.

"Thanks a lot, Gramps. I'm not planning to seduce you. I just need a little cover until things quiet down. I'm not in the game. I'm a reporter. I think I've upset someone, and he's sent people to suggest that I lay off. If they find me, I'll probably get a whack or two, but I doubt it will be much worse."

The food arrives and I swipe a few French fries while she chomps on the sandwich.

"Come on," I say. "The big bad wolf is after you and you choose a very senior senior for protection? Next, you'll be telling me what great big teeth I have. What do you really want? How did you know I am here?"

I know that my name and fame are well-known in certain circles and very often I am accosted by reporters who want to know about my latest adventure. My latest adventure is more than two years old. I pretend that I'm retired these days while I wait for something, anything, to happen. Maybe this is it.

To be honest, I do look more like somebody's Grampa. I'm not wearing a mask, of course, at the table. My curly locks have long ago retreated to give me the high forehead that denotes either high intelligence or wisdom. I forget which. I am wearing a golfer's shirt and a casual, green sweater. My face with its wrinkles and smile lines reveals my many years kicking around Canada. I'm 88 and look it.

"Tell me a little about yourself, Kate. Who are you? What do you want? Are you really in any kind of trouble or is this just a novel approach you are trying?"

"I'm Mandisa Katherine Ngobani, originally from Zimbabwe but here in Canada via South Africa."

She pronounces 'Ngobani' as "Ing-go-bay-knee", so I query her and ask her spell it out. She goes on.

"Mandisa means 'sweet' and I'm just a sweet person. Katherine means 'pure' and it comes from the Greek.

Your suggestion that I'm a hooker is not only an affront, but also it's offensive," she says.

"You're being redundant," I tell her. "Affront means offensive."

As a professional writer, I take umbrage over redundancy.

She ignores me and goes on with her introduction.

"In Zulu, Ngobani represents ambition, independence, strength, reliability, determination, and professionalism. All in all, I'm a sweet, pure, ambitious professional. My nickname is Kate so you can call me that."

"I'm almost sorry I asked," I say. "Do you work or are you a lady of leisure?"

"I'm an investigative reporter for the CBC and ordinarily I work with a partner who is managing this assignment. He didn't show up at the office where we are to meet. Rather foolishly, I went ahead without him and tried to do the interview. They took offense at some of my questions, so I stopped the interview and scooted. As my taxi pulled away, several people followed me out of his building, but I think I lost them."

"Do you know who I am?" I ask.

"You're Grampa Bill, a very generous old guy sitting alone in the nearest restaurant I could find when I left the taxi."

"Kate, Kate, Kate... We will need to have a long talk when you've finished your coffee. Would you trust me enough to come up to my room? We need to talk."

"I think I could take you rather easily if you decide to try anything foolish. Sure," she says as she drains the last of the coffee, "lead the way."

I pay and we go to the elevator and up to my third-floor room.

Kate tosses her jacket on the bed and sits in the one comfortable chair. She looks up at me and smiles.

"Okay, Bill. Who are you?"

"You are in my chair," I point out.

"Sorry. You want me on the bed?"

"On the bed, not in it."

She gets up, spins around, and plunks herself down on the end of the bed. I take my proper place in the chair. She looks at me rather curiously.

"Well," she says.

Although the Bayshore Inn provides a decent King-size bed, the room is hardly first class. There is a TV and a tray with a couple of glasses protected by paper wrapping, but they don't sport a drinks cabinet. There is a coffee maker of sorts.

"Would you like a drink of anything before we begin?" I ask.

"Get on with it," she says. "Who did I happen to find? What's your name, Bill?"

"Jenkins," I say.

"Should I know you?" she asks.

"You certainly should. You picked me out to harass tonight. Don't kid me. Do you remember "The Case of the Ancient American," I say, knowing that this will clear everything up.

"Are you talking about old Trump?"

"The Case of the Brainy Birds," I add.

"I don't get it. Brainy Birds? Do you mean Smart Gals?"

"The Case of the Cannabis Cat," I say, trying to clarify her confusion.

It doesn't seem to help. She looks as puzzled as ever.

"These cases are all sited in Charlestown, just 75 kilometers east of here," I explain.

"Cases? Are you, or maybe I should say, were you a policeman? Are these cases you've handled? I'm afraid what's happening is that you are remembering things that happened in the distant past. It often occurs when you get older; you forget lots of everyday things and you remember what happened years ago."

She looks around the room, possibly wondering what her chances are if she must leave suddenly.

"Maybe things have cooled off enough now and I should shove off," she says.

She reaches back for her jacket and gets to her feet.

"Bill, you've been a great help, but I think I'll call it a night and head home. It was nice meeting you."

She isn't going to get away that easily.

"The Case of the Diligent Detective," I blurt out. "The Electrified Envoy, The Forgotten Fort, The Greedy Goat."

She heads for the door, but I cut her off.

"There's one more: The Hidden Hound," I say, "and now, at last, The Case of the Intrepid Investigator. Go and sit down," I order.

Rather meekly, she lays her jacket on the bed and sits down again. It is time for the great revelation.

"I'm a writer," I confess. "Those are the titles of the eight books I've written and published. As you can tell, each successive title uses the next letter of the alphabet. I've been suffering from writer's block for years because I couldn't find a suitable 'I' title. You have solved it. The Case of the Intrepid Investigator. You are my saviour."

Kate seems a little worried as I reveal my identity and profession. She probably has not spoken with a famous author before and perhaps that rattles her.

"Well, that's nice, Bill. I'm sure you'll be able to write a good story with that title. I'm happy for you," she says as she checks her watch.

"Gosh! Look at the time! I'd better get going," she decides as she stands up again.

"Not so fast, Kate. We must talk. I need to know more about this investigation. Where are you staying?"

She admits to living in an apartment on nearby Front Street.

"Kate! I have it! I'll move in with you and be your writer-in-residence. I'm rather tired of the Bayshore Inn anyway," I say as I go to the closet, pulling out my bag and laptop.

"Let's go!"

"But..." is all she says.

It is an unusual start to my next adventure.

Chapter 2

Kate seems speechless when I check out of the Bayshore Inn. I presume she isn't used to a take-charge guy. She tries interjecting a couple of "buts" as I hustle her out of the hotel and up to Front Street, but she finally gives up.

"You'll see why this isn't a good idea when we get there," she manages to say.

I stay strong and silent as we walk the half-dozen blocks to her building. The sign on the building says: 'The Factory', but clearly it is an apartment building and a very classy one at that.

It is the third or fourth residence along Front Street. We pass a senior's residence, a high condo building and one with a sign saying: 'Carson Landing'. Two more high rise buildings sit on the property on the shore of Lake Iroquois behind Carson Landing. One is quite lit up and is a Marriott hotel.

Kate puts on her mask and I follow suit as we enter. All buildings in Linden have a big sign at the entrance saying "Masks Required" so wearing a mask has become a habit for everyone. She leads me to the two elevators and presses the "UP" button. The door on the left one opens almost immediately.

"I'm on ten," she says as the door closes.

Her apartment is directly opposite the elevator and with a quick turn of a key, we are in.

"This won't work," says Kate. "I just moved here and the only furniture I have is an air mattress. It's a single bed. I am planning on getting more stuff tomorrow. As you can see, it's a nice spacious place, but I think you're going to have to return to the Bayshore Inn."

It is certainly spacious. The entrance hallway passes a den on the left and then opens into a 25 by 15-foot living room. A large bedroom parallels the living room, but because the only furniture in it is a single bed, it looks cavernous as well. At the far end of each room, the wall is glass, looking out on Front Street.

"Well, I have some furniture in storage. I can get it in here tomorrow and that will save you spending your money. It takes about three months to write one of my adventures, so I'll be out of your hair by the end of February."

"Why don't you head back to the hotel and we can chat about this tomorrow. Could I meet you in the restaurant for breakfast? How about eight o'clock?" Kate suggests.

"No, no, Kate. The lack of a bed doesn't bother me. I can spread a few of my clothes from this bag on the floor in that room by the entrance. You needn't worry about me. I've slept in rougher places."

Kate straightens up and looks me in the eye. Our masks are pocketed and the look on her face is rather determined.

"Maybe I don't make myself clear, Bill. You've rushed us here and haven't given me a chance to say 'No' to this idea. It's not on. I'm not shacking up with you, a crazy old writer. This is my apartment; this is my say. I think you are relatively harmless, certainly in comparison with the gangsters I'm investigating, but I don't really care whether you write up this case. I've got a job to do and it doesn't include you."

It strikes me as unusual that Kate expresses her objection to my modest proposal so forcefully. Naturally, I need to plead my case.

"It included me at nine o'clock when you are in trouble," I point out. C'mon, Kate. Humour an old man. I won't tell anyone we're sharing accommodation. I'll just sit at my desk and type away during the day while you investigate. At night you can tell me how the day went."

"Next you'll be offering to do the cooking and washing up."

Her sarcasm is evident. I go along with it, trying not to argue.

"Sure, and I make beds, dust, sweep floors. I'll be your man Friday."

8

"What part of 'No' do you not understand? If you want to fight and stay here by force, I doubt that you can win that battle. There's the door. Out you go."

She obviously needs training in negotiating. You must give a little to get a little. I walk over to the window and look down on Front Street. A car goes by and I don't hear a sound.

"This place is really quiet," I say. "I can get a lot of work done during the day while you are out investigating. How about a compromise? I'll go back to the hotel tonight, but tomorrow I'll lend you enough of my furniture to make the place habitable. I'll move my furniture in here and I'll give you a written promise that I will move out with all my furniture on Feb 28th. How does that sound?"

"How does 'No' sound?" she replies.

"You are a stubborn woman," I observe, "pretty, but stubborn. How much would you want me to pay in addition? I can cover the rent. I can give you half of the royalties on the book sales. I can make you a co-author and you can become as famous as I am. What can I offer that will change your mind?"

"Okay, I'll tell you what, Bill," she replies. "If you will go back to the hotel now, I will think about it overnight and meet you at the restaurant at 12 noon tomorrow. I must discuss this with my CBC partner."

As she goes on, I can see she is giving a little.

"I will draw up the conditions for us to live together while you write your story. If the conditions are acceptable, it's 'Yes'. How does that sound? It is better than 'No', I think."

I am reluctant to accept this plan, but I realize she isn't going to budge. I walk towards her and offer a handshake to seal the deal.

"I agree," I say.

She steps back.

"No handshakes. We're bumping elbows now," she says.

"May I leave my laptop here overnight. It's silly to lug it back to the hotel. Would that be okay?" I ask.

I am trying the old 'get the nose in the tent' trick. The laptop will be followed by a couple of rooms of furniture. I can use the morning to load a rental truck and move in by the afternoon.

"Okay, put it in the den. That's the room by the front door," she says.

There are doors with panes of glass from top to bottom revealing the den. I turn on the light, open the door and set my laptop against the wall. Kate stands between me and the rest of the apartment with my suitcase in her hand. I almost get the fleeting idea that she might shove me out the door and toss the bag after me. I note that she is as big as I am and can probably drop me on the floor and sit on my head until I agree to her insane demands. Graciously, I take the bag and turn to the door.

"I'll see you tomorrow at noon, then. Have a good sleep," I say as I step into the hallway towards the elevator.

After she closes the door, I hear a click that might indicate that she'd thrown the lock on the door. Funnily enough, she doesn't say "Goodnight" or "See you then", but of course, I realize that people in their twenties have not had the benefit of manners taught to them in childhood the way we more mature seniors have.

I press the "DOWN" button and wait for the elevator.

The receptionist at the Bayshore Inn half-smiles and comments that maybe things haven't worked out when I register for another night there. I don't reply; I simply sign the papers she places on the counter, take my plastic room key card, and go to the elevator. At least she doesn't put me back in the same room.

Chapter 3

I am up at 8 a.m. and eating breakfast by 9. I know it will be a busy day, so I have a full breakfast with a couple of eggs over easy, bacon, hash browns, O.J., and coffee. There isn't a paper, but I check my emails and look at the CBC headlines on their news channel. Trump is refusing to concede so I switch over to CNN to get an unbiased report of the situation.

The restaurant isn't busy. The covid pandemic has cut into their business. Remembering the rather unusual events of the night before, I check out the other diners in case one of them is following up on the pursuit of Kate. A man in a grey business suit finishes his breakfast and as he is leaving, offers me his newspaper.

"I've read it all," he says. "Just the usual news."

I am unsure of his motive, but I decline, keeping to the side of caution. I did notice that he is wearing brown slip-on shoes and they don't seem to go with his other business attire.

'You can't tell the gangsters from regular businessmen these days,' I think.

I sign the breakfast bill, go back to the room, and start phoning. The Get Smart storage people say it will be okay to take some of my belongings out this afternoon. The Hertz truck rental doesn't have anything available, but luckily Discount has a five-ton truck they can let me have after 3 p.m. I figure that will work. I'll take a taxi out to Discount so that I won't have to worry about the car. Now, I need to find two strong men to do the heavy lifting.

There is a 'Temp Workers' listing on the Internet, but they don't answer the phone. After several tries, I find a moving company who will assign two men to the task. I arrange to pick them up at 3:30.

I check over my 'Things to do' list and add 'Check out before 11 a.m.'

I sit in the restaurant drinking one cup of coffee after another from 10:50 when I check out, until 12:30.

'Kate must be busy,' I think.

Then, a taxi driver walks in and the gal acting as 'Maitre D', directs him to me. He is carrying my laptop.

"Mr. Jenkins?" he asks.

"That's me," I acknowledge, as a sinking feeling strikes my chest.

"Miss Ngobani is called away on business. She asked me to take this laptop to you. It is yours, isn't it?"

I reach for my wallet and give him a fiver.

"Thanks very much," I say.

He tips his cap, turns, and leaves.

I finish my coffee, pay the check, deposit my bag and laptop in the luggage room, and head out. I am damned if I'll check into the Bayshore Inn again.

I trace my steps towards 'The Factory', wanting to verify that her returning my laptop isn't a ruse. Kate is probably just having second thoughts and needs a little more persuasion. When I get to the vestibule, I use the display system to find the code to ring her apartment. Unfortunately, Ngobani doesn't turn up in the list of residents. I try the Superintendent and he answers.

"Hi," I start, "I'm looking for Miss Ngobani. I can't find her on the list of residents."

"She left," he says, rather succinctly.

"But she was here last night."

"She was a temporary," he says. "If you want her forwarding address, you'll have to go to the Parker rental office in the next building, 'Carson Landing'. They have all the information."

12

I thank him and hit 'Cancel'.

It is only a short walk back to 'Carson Landing', but it is a chilly day, and the wind is blowing. I pull on the rental office door. It won't open. There are a couple of people inside, a man at the counter and a lady presumably serving him. I knock on the door and the lady comes over and opens the door.

"Sorry, only one person at a time due to covid."

"Right," I reply.

I walk a few steps away around the corner out of the wind and wait. I remember from my earlier days in Linden, that the windy city is known for world class sailing. They hold regattas here every summer and spectators line up along the shore of Lake Iroquois to enjoy the view.

Linden is a university town, with Champlain University and its 25,000 students flooding in from September to May. It is also a retirement destination because the cost of homes is considerably lower than those in Toronto or Vancouver.

Front Street is a wall of apartment buildings, but the streets to the west for blocks are single family residences, many where they rent rooms to students. It is a quiet, windy place.

After about ten minutes, the man leaves, and I am allowed in.

"I'm looking for the forwarding address for a Miss Ngobani who has been staying in 'The Factory'. Do you have it?" I ask.

"I'm sorry, I'm not allowed to give out that information. Does she know how to contact you?"

The lady seems a little severe for someone serving the public. I'm making a reasonable request.

"No. I've moved out of the Bayshore Inn," I say.

"Does she have your cell number?"

"I'm afraid not."

"Unless you are related to her, I'm afraid you will just have to contact her employer. Do you know where she works?"

"I think she is doing project work here in Linden," I reply.

"I'm sorry. I really can't help you. If you'll excuse me, I must start the rental process on her apartment. We have so many buildings, there's always a ton of work to do."

"Did you say you plan to rent out her apartment?"

"Of course. That's what we do here," implying, I imagine, that everyone would know what a rental office does.

"How much is the rent? I might be interested," I say.

I end up in the apartment that night, with furniture, many boxes of treasures, but no air mattress. Kate must have taken it with her.

The movers are careful and efficient. The superintendent dedicates an elevator, and the truck is empty in a couple of hours. I return it to Discount, take a taxi to my new home and sleep the sleep of the innocent.

Chapter 4

I am in dismay when I look in the den the next morning and see how many boxes are waiting to be unpacked.

I have all my clothes and a few other essentials. I don't have any food and I don't want to go back to the Bayshore Inn for breakfast again. After a quick shower, I drive to a supermarket, Parker Foods, about ten blocks away, and get enough supplies to last a week or two.

It takes four trips from my parking spot #4 behind the building to the locked back door which opens with a key fob. I wait for the elevator, ride up to my floor, get in my apartment, stow the food, wait for the elevator, and return to the car to get the next load. I begin to question the idea of living in a high rise by the time everything is put away.

I treat myself to Shreddies for breakfast as I haven't found the cookware yet. Then I return to the unpacking chores. By supper time I am down to about ten boxes to be cleared. One holds pictures and paintings so it can wait. My china, wine glasses, pots and pans, and cutlery are all in their appropriate cupboards. I decide to stop for my first supper in my new digs.

I fry a steak with the burner on high and set off a smoke alarm. I grab a dishtowel to swing under the smoke detector to get the alarm off in fear of having firemen arrive. I hope that the Super, Rick, doesn't hear about it and report it to everyone. Usually, I try to keep a low profile, except when I'm promoting one of my books, because a writer is a preferred, quiet tenant.

I boil a potato, some frozen peas and select a plastic container of chocolate pudding as my gourmet dessert.

As I sit at the old kitchen table, I wonder how I will ever get in touch with my investigator. My mind flits from thought to thought. Has she really been called away? Perhaps the gangsters, she never did tell me who they are, captured her and are torturing her in the basement of their building.

Tomorrow, I decide, I'll call the CBC in Ottawa and see if she has simply gone back to report on her work so far. I consider all possibilities and vow to take up her cause if she has been murdered.

On reconsidering, I realize that maybe it would be easier to change the title of my story. I go over the many double 'I' words I have tried in the past:

Ignorant Indian (no, too racist)

Important Issues (no, too generic)

Ingenious Inkling (no, too vague)

Idiot's Idiosyncrasy (no, too many letters)

Inept Imbecile (no, too anti-American).

No matter how you slice it, an adventurous (intrepid) person who investigates crimes and criminals gets my vote. I'll just have to find my investigator.

The next morning, after giving the CBC and myself time to have a 'wake-me-up' coffee, I check the number for CBC Ottawa and give them a call. After listening to the standard message about how things take longer because of that world-wide pandemic that I may have heard about on their news broadcasts, and several messages about important people with whom I might wish to speak, I hit '0' and get a real person.

"Could I speak with Miss Kate Ngobani, please."

"What department is she with?" she asks.

"Investigative reporting," I answer.

"That's not a department. It's what we all do. Is she in TV or Radio, English or French?"

"I think she's African," I say. "Probably in TV."

"We don't have an African network, only English or French."

"Oh! I see. That would be English."

"Sorry," says the operator. "We don't have anyone by that name on staff."

"She might be a contractor," I suggest.

"Well," she replied, "then she wouldn't have a phone extension, would she? Do you have her cell? You should just call her directly," she advises.

"Thank you," I say and click the red button.

'Now what,' I wonder.

Then I have a brilliant idea. What if I write the story about myself, me investigating the person who is claiming to be an investigative reporter? Intrepid means fearless as well as adventurous. I might be walking into a lion's den, but I tend to be fearless and adventurous, especially when it comes to literary things. I spend half my waking hours reading whodunits from the library.

I would become the Intrepid Investigator, revealing only on the last page that I am the Intrepid one. (Note to self: If this works, I must put this paragraph at the end of the last chapter where I reveal the solution to the mystery.)

I am new to today's Linden. I lived here as a student and later as a worker in my chosen field of Information Technology, a fancy term for a "computer guy". From my student days I know about the pizza restaurants that will include a few illegal drugs with the pizza if I say the right words and am willing to pay for an expensive pizza. I know that taxi drivers will deliver beer after hours.

However, the world has moved on. The modern gangster probably runs a few legal businesses through which he can launder drug money. And, sad to say, human trafficking is rampant everywhere.

I have no idea where to start or what the gangsters are doing these days. Perhaps I need a professional investigator.

I google for 'Investigators' and find 219 million hits. I try 'Jenkins Investigators' and cut the list down to eight million prospects. Finally, I find 'First Investigators'.

They sound professional and they promise to be discreet. They are in Ottawa. I save their number just in case.

I think of dropping in at the police station and asking who the big gangsters are these days, but they will probably be less helpful than the Parker rental office and provide me with free room and board until I confess to something.

It is approaching 9 p.m. and I remember that it is about the time I'd met Kate for the first time. I suddenly think 'What if Kate has switched to the Bayshore Inn?'

I know it is a ridiculous idea, a bit of a long shot, but I throw on a jacket, walk over to the Bayshore Inn and sneak in past the lobby. Sure enough, there is Kate, sitting by herself in a relatively empty section of the restaurant.

I sit down opposite her and simply say "Pretend I'm with you."

"I'm Kate," she says, and I reply 'Bill'.

"Would you like a coffee or something to eat?" she asks.

"I would say a sandwich and a coffee, please, but I'm not hungry. This is like déjà vu all over again," I say. "What's new with you?"

"Nothing I want to talk about, especially in public," she says. "How about you?"

"I got a new apartment," I brag. "I've moved in already. It's nearby. Want to see it? Maybe we can patch up any old misunderstandings."

"Sure. Why not. There's nothing happening here," she replies.

I let her pay her tab and we head out to Main Street and turn left onto Front. When we approach 'The Factory', she starts to laugh.

"You're right," I say. "I'm in your old apartment building."

We go in, up to the tenth floor and I unlock apartment 1001. Kate walks in and turns on the lights.

"Holy Cow! This place looks great with some furniture in it."

"They rented it to me when I heard that you weren't coming back. I even got a free Alexa and Wi-Fi to go with the apartment. I still have a few boxes to unpack," I say. "It is fine for now. The couch makes out into a bed, so you are welcome to stay here rather than in that sterile Bayshore Inn."

"Thanks, but I'm probably going to leave Linden. The investigation has taken a bad turn."

"Oh? Are the gangsters after you again?"

"No, it's much worse than that. My partner in this investigation, Ted Simmons, has not returned to his room in the Westside Motel. He didn't check out; he just hasn't shown up. He's not in Ottawa, his home base. He may be afraid and has bailed out, but I think even then he would have tried to contact me."

"But you moved too. He may be having trouble contacting you," I suggest.

"No. We have several backup procedures. He hasn't phoned or shown up at any of our rendezvous sites. I'm worried that maybe he went in alone as I did. Maybe they caught him in a lie and grabbed him."

"Did he have a cameraman with him? Surely they wouldn't try anything with a cameraman shooting the scene."

'We use hidden cameras. He would be capturing everything in a small camera either in his clothing or in his briefcase. Why he didn't wait for me, I'll never know. I wasn't late getting there."

"Are you in the Bayshore Inn now?"

"Yes."

"There's no point in going back and checking out now. You can check out tomorrow before 11 a.m. It will cost the same. You look exhausted. Let me show you the hideabed."

I walk to the couch and easily convert it into a bed by lifting a tab on the front. I push the back down and toss the big cushions onto a nearby rocking chair.

"I'll get you some sheets," I say as I walk to my bedroom to the linen closet.

I return in ten seconds with two Queen-size sheets and a couple of pillows. Kate helps by making the bed while I find a comforter for her.

I point to the bathroom and say I'll get her some PJ's.

"There's a bathrobe hanging on the door you can use," I say, as I head to my dresser and dig out a second set of pajamas.

"These may be a little big, but we're practically the same size," I tell her.

I hand her the PJ's, turn off most of the lights and retreat to my bedroom.

The bathroom has a door leading to my bedroom and another leading to the living room. Kate chooses the living room and climbs into bed. I use the bathroom, take my usual night pills, hang up my clothes and go out to the living room to turn out the last light.

"Have a good sleep, Kate. Tomorrow we'll find Ted and decide what to do." I click off the light. Kate says "Mmm". I retreat to my room, close the door, slide into bed, and turn off the lamp beside my bed.

Usually, I fall asleep within ten to fifteen minutes, but I can't seem to drift off. My thoughts about Ted, about Kate, about my new apartment, even what we will have for breakfast, keep swirling around. I try turning on my left side, lying on my back, turning on my right side. Nothing works. Finally, I start counting each breath and that works.

I wake up at 4 a.m. needing to pee, one of the joys of old age, and turn on the light. I use the bathroom and creep back to bed, douse the light, and try to remember what I've been dreaming. Usually, if I can remember where I am in the dream, I can drift back to sleep easily and quickly.

Nothing works this time. I lie awake until 7 a.m. when I decide I might as well get up. I gather some clothes, go to the bathroom, and shave, shower, and dress. I make my bed and head for the kitchen to prepare some breakfast for my guest and myself.

Kate is gone! The sofa is back being a sofa; the bed clothes and pillows sit carefully on the rocking chair. There is no note, but at least the door keys are in the hallway dish and the door is unlocked.

Chapter 5

It is easy to understand her aberrant behaviour. The poor girl probably finds the sofa bed too hard compared to her usual air mattress. She doesn't have pen and paper to leave a note. She worries about Ted and wants to get an early start looking for him. Perhaps she worries that spending a night in the apartment with a strange man will hurt her reputation.

Later, I find out that Kate agrees with everything I say to avoid another big argument with me as on Sunday night. She is exhausted and intends to return to the Bayshore Inn as soon as she is sure I am asleep. That's what happens.

I am certain that Kate will be back, perhaps lugging her air mattress with her, so I go ahead and eat breakfast. Then, I turn to the boxes that I need to empty and end up hanging all the pictures. The apartment is beginning to look like home.

Time for a break.

I turn on the kettle for a coffee and the TV to get caught up on the news. I like instant coffee, so as the TV warms up, I add hot water to my spoonful of instant and settle on the couch. A little searching with the remote brings up the local news channel where I see an overhead shot, probably from a drone hovering over the bridge to the east. An ambulance and a couple of squad cars are blocking traffic that stretch all the way up the hill to the east and back over the lift bridge to Front Street. Paramedics are wrestling a stretcher up the bank from the water while several police officers wander around. Clearly, there has been an accident on the bridge with someone injured.

I switch to CNN and see that Trump is continuing to refuse to concede the election. Now he is sending lawyers to every state where he has a chance to have some Democratic votes ruled illegal. I wonder what part of 'No' he doesn't understand; then decide not to criticize him after remembering Kate has asked me that same question.

I go to the window and see that the lineup of cars caused by the problem at the bridge stretches way beyond this building. The problem has obviously been going on for some time. It is 1:30 p.m. and the TV is turning to commercials, so I switch it off.

'Where the Hell is Kate?' I wonder. I know that she must check out by 11:00 a.m.

I make a tomato sandwich for lunch and heat another coffee. As I sit at the table, I decide to leave a note in the lobby for Kate in case she shows up while I am out. I'll take a pair of trousers to the dry cleaners, Hillary's, on Wellington, a couple of blocks from the bridge. I'll swing by and check out the accident and maybe drop into the Bayshore Inn to see if Kate did check out this morning.

However, by the time I leave Hillary's, the traffic is moving on Front and I skip the accident scene. Kate has indeed checked out of the Bayshore Inn. She is not in their restaurant either, so I return to 'The Factory' and retrieve my note.

I am at loose ends. I don't feel like watching TV. I have nothing to read. I am a little tired from the early morning and the long walk, so I stretch out on the bed for a short nap.

The cell rings, waking me up. I say 'Hello' a few times and then realize it is someone at the door. I press '9' to let her in. It must be Kate. No one else knows about my new apartment.

I go to the door and wait for the elevator. When it arrives, out steps a weeping Kate. She carries her bag and the box holding her air mattress. I take the box and lead her in. When the door closes behind her, she drops her small suitcase and gives me a big hug, breaking into sobs.

I know she is feeling badly about having left me in the night. I pat her on the back and say "It's okay. I understand. I'm glad you came back."

She breaks off the hug, wipes her eyes, and blurts out "They found his body floating in the lake near the bridge. They killed him, the bastards."

I lead her over to the couch and say: "I'll put on a coffee."

I notice that it is 5:30 p.m. I guess my short nap has been for three solid hours. I find a package of Kleenex and set it on the coffee table. I really don't know what to do.

"Are you sure?" I ask. "How do you know it is Ted there at the bridge?"

She takes a Kleenex and blows her nose not very delicately.

"I phoned Ottawa this morning and they haven't heard from him. I tried everyone I know. Then I checked out, leaving my bag and the box in the luggage room. I took a taxi to the police station on Norton Street and reported him missing. I told them that I saw him last on Saturday and he'd missed a meeting with me on Sunday. I filled out their missing persons report form and handed it in. Then I went to lunch and heard about his body in the lake."

She pauses to get her breathe. I try to get in a word.

"Maybe he'll turn up with a big apology. Don't give up hope until you know for sure."

"I know for sure. The police called me. I'll go and identify his body tomorrow morning. I'm sure it's Ted. They killed him. I came here because I want you to go with me. I don't know anyone else in Linden."

"It might have been an accident. What makes you sure that someone killed him?" I ask.

"People don't go swimming in Lake Iroquois in November. How could it be an accident?"

"Did you phone the CBC?" I ask.

"The police did. They couldn't get much information because he's a contractor, not an employee. They did get his address in Ottawa, but that's about all."

"You've had an awful time. You must have been pretty close to Ted," I say. "Would you like a drink? I have some Scotch. Let's have a shot. Maybe that will help."

We have a drink or two and I put a meal together. By eight o'clock we are both feeling a little better and have switched to dry, red wine.

"I don't know what I'm going to do. This is a good contract. I hope to come to the CBC's attention and perhaps get chosen to be a full-time employee. I don't want to go back to Toronto. There's too much covid there."

I know she isn't looking for answers. I try to avoid providing solutions to other people's problems. She needs sympathy tonight and will figure out what to do when the shock of Ted's death has receded.

"Another glass of vino?" I ask.

"Sure."

"Have you heard about Trump?" I ask.

"He lost," she says.

"Yes, but he's refusing to concede. He's suing everyone he can think of and is not cooperating with the transition procedures," I report.

"Oh well, I imagine the Americans will work it out. They always seem to be able to muddle through," she says. "It's not like Zimbabwe where I was brought up or South Africa where I lived for a few years before I emigrated to Canada."

"When did you come here?" I ask.

"A year ago, September 12th. It took two years to get approval and I left my daughter behind with my sister."

"You left your daughter? I didn't even know you are married," I comment. "How old is she?"

"She's just eight. I'm not married, though. My partner became abusive. I left him and began teaching school in Rustenburg, South Africa. When I get established, I'll send for my daughter. Of course, nothing will change until covid-19 is under control and the border is open again."

"My gosh, Kate. You look as though you are in your low twenties. You must be older than that unless you had your kid in high school."

"I'm 32. I finished a B. Comm. degree in 2012. I was on an accounting contract in Toronto when this investigation came along. I like the idea of the work and the pay too. How old are you, old Bill?"

"Funny you should call me that. My handle on Skype is 'goodoldbill'. I was 88 in July. My wife died in 2019 in BC and I decided to move back east. I've been writing and publishing for eight years, mainly as a hobby. I used to work as a computer guy."

"You seem pretty keen on writing up this investigation. Does it really matter to you?"

"Well, my next story has to be "The Case of the I-something I-something and I think Intrepid Investigator is perfect. I suppose if you stop being an investigator, I'll have to change it to "The Case of the Inky Intern" and make you an author-in-training. Do you mind that I'm using your name? Would you rather I choose a different name for my heroine?"

"Am I the heroine in your story? That's different. If I'm not the butt of your feeble jokes, I guess it's okay. Will I get some of the royalties?"

"Regrettably, my books don't sell well so there aren't any royalties to speak of," I confess.

Somehow or other I've managed to get off the topic of Ted's death. Since it is after 10 p.m., I think it is time to get some sleep.

"I'll make up the bed for you again as long as you promise not to run back to the Bayshore Inn in the middle of the night. Promise?"

"I guess so. I'm out of the hotel and your sofa bed is quite comfortable."

"I can blow up your air mattress if you'd prefer that," I offer.

"No. I'll go with the sofa bed. I see the sheets and PJ's are still out," she says.

She stands up and starts taking the big cushions off the sofa. I get the sheets and comforter from the rocking chair and together we make the bed up again. She opens her suitcase and sets it near the window.

"You go first," I say. "I'll tidy up the kitchen while you get ready in the bathroom."

She is quick, but I have everything in the dishwasher before she is ready. I leave just one light burning and head to my room. When she leaves the bathroom, I go through my routine and before long I am in my bed with the lights out. The light goes out in the living room soon after.

At about 2 a.m., Kate wakes me up as she crawls into bed with me.

"I won't attack you," she promises. "Can you just hold me for a little while."

I roll towards her and hold her close as she sobs. After a few minutes, she calms down and breaks the embrace.

"Thanks," she murmurs. "I think I can sleep now."

I roll away from her and she puts one arm around me, snuggling up. She sleeps and I don't for quite a long time. When I wake up in the morning, she isn't there. I check and find her back in the sofa bed.

'Well,' I think, 'at least she hasn't run away.'

I have my usual shave and shower, but rather than wake her up by working in the kitchen, I move to my laptop on my desk and begin writing. I start with the header "The Case of the Intrepid Investigator". You must admit that I'm an optimist.

Chapter 6

We are having a quiet breakfast when Kate's phone rings. She listens for a minute and then agrees to whatever her caller requests.

"Yes. I'll be there at 10:30," she says.

"The police, a Detective Thomson," she reports. "After I identify Ted's remains, he wants to talk about what Ted and I were doing. You will give me a lift there, right? He wants me there at 10:30."

"No problem," I say. "I can wait for you. The son of an old pal of mine works there so I can chat with him and let him know I'm back in Linden."

"I don't know how long I'll be, but as far as I'm concerned, I'll stay as long as they need me. I hope we can find out who killed Ted and if his murder was ordered by the gangster we are trying to interview."

"Who is this gangster, anyway?" I ask, not really expecting her to name him.

"He's the general manager of the real estate company, Parker. His name is George Kirkman. His name was Giorgi Kastikoff back in Russia. He came to Canada in his twenties. He made a fortune in some software company and is now managing Parker. Ted thought that maybe he's importing girls from Eastern European countries and drugs from Mexico, though covid-19 has probably cramped his style with the borders closed and special scrutiny on all air passengers. I really don't know much yet."

"I think Parker manages apartment buildings. There's a sign in front of this building saying 'Parker'," I say. "Kirkman must be doing pretty well. I haven't seen any strip clubs called Parker, but he could be running girls out of classy apartment buildings like this one. Maybe he's a silent partner in the illegal stuff. He sounds like the sort of person you should avoid. What were the CBC thinking when they decided to investigate him? They usually don't go after Russian Mafia, do they?" I ask.

"It was Ted. He went to the CBC with a detailed proposal based on something he'd heard in Toronto. He got a conditional contract. CBC paid us for the first month. If we come up with something interesting, they will go for a much bigger deal. We don't really have any evidence, just hearsay and rumours so far. I hope it's enough to get the police to take it seriously."

"They take murder pretty seriously, Kate. I'm sure they will look into it thoroughly," I comment.

At 10:20 we pull out of my parking spot and head to Mackenzie Street. Linden is small enough that you can get almost anywhere in ten minutes. The traffic is light. We are stuck behind a bus going out Norton towards the Police Headquarters. I catch a red light about 200 yards short of the building, but I am not concerned that we might be late.

As we get close, I check my rear mirror and see no one in the right lane. As I look ahead for the entrance, luckily, I glance to the left as a car enters Norton from a side street. It comes out aggressively, just missing whapping us from the left because I goose the gas. The driver must be in a hurry. He pulls up close behind us, and I speed up a bit. Then, a car coming towards us along Norton suddenly swerves into our lane, trying to pass a truck.

My reflexes are still surprisingly good, and I cut sharply to the right. The car whizzes by us but catches the one following close behind us. There is a terrific crash as I turn in to the driveway for the police station.

"Good God," Kate says. "That was close. I hope no one is hurt."

As we get out and survey the scene, we can see that neither driver has exited their car. Traffic slams to a stop in both directions. I hurry Kate into the station and tell the officer behind the protective glass cage that there has been an accident out in front. After he summons some officers to handle the accident scene, he asks us how he can help.

Kate replies: "I'm Kate Ngobani, here for a 10:30 meeting with Detective Thomson."

We don't wait long. I decide to watch the police handle the accident while Thomson takes Kate off for the identification chore and her interview. Since I haven't met Ted, I could hardly identify him.

Before long there is a fire engine, ambulance and a tow truck blocking outbound Norton Street. Police direct traffic, paramedics work on one guy on the ground and police interview another man. I don't go near them, just watch from the safety of the police station.

By the time Kate returns, the accident has been cleared. One man went off in the ambulance, tow trucks removed the damaged cars, and the man being questioned has disappeared.

"How did it go?" I ask.

"It isn't Ted," she says. "The guy is about Ted's age, but he drowned. They think it happened further up the Reesor River a few days ago. No one else has been reported missing so they will publicize it and see if anyone comes forward with information. What a relief it is! I still can't understand why Ted hasn't got in touch."

She went on to describe the interview.

"With the detective, I tell them everything about three times. They must be stupid. I don't hold out much hope for them finding Ted," she reports.

"They do that not because they are stupid, Kate. They just want to be sure you keep saying the same details. If you are lying, you won't be able to keep your lies straight. If you are telling the truth, as I'm sure you are, they just want you to repeat it," I explain.

"Oh. Well, they asked for the proposal that Ted has prepared for the CBC, but they'll have to get that from the CBC. I understand that Ottawa police have checked his apartment and the local police have emptied his room at the Westside Motel.

I told them what we suspect about Mr. Kirkman and they made some comment about amateurs by which I suppose they meant Ted and me. They say that Parker is a long-established Linden company with a sterling reputation. You are right about them managing apartment buildings. They own them and provide all sorts of services.

How is the son of your friend you want to see?" she asks.

"He isn't on duty. I just watched the police handle the accident," I reply.

"That's the first accident I've ever seen in Canada. In South Africa, there are lots and lots of accidents. The drivers are either drunk or careless. In Canada, the drivers seem to be more careful. The one who nearly hit us was going fast. Was he trying to pass someone, do you think?"

"Probably something like that," I say.

We go to the car and drive downtown. I park outside Welcome Mobile on Mackenzie Street and tell Kate to wait as I'd be just a minute. I'm back ten minutes later with two new cell phones and we head back to 'The Factory'.

When we get inside, I ask Kate for her cell phone.

"You just bought a new one," she says.

"Never mind," I say. "Let me see yours."

She hands it to me. I examine it closely before setting it on the table.

"What's with the phone?" she asks.

"I think it is bugged," I say. "How do you think Kirkman knows we are heading to the police station? That little accident was an assassination attempt that failed. Thank God I've still got the reflexes I had in the Air Force. If I hadn't dodged that car coming at us, you wouldn't be chatting with Detective Thomson; you'd be lying in the morgue," I explain. "If the so-called accident didn't kill us, you can be sure that one of the drivers would have finished us off.

I'm not ready to die," I add. "I have a book to write."

Kate took it all in, but she did have one question for me.

31

"Do you still have some of that Scotch handy?"

Chapter 7

"We've got to get out of here," I tell Kate over a Scotch on the Rocks.

"Why? Aren't we safe? Nobody could get us here."

"Well, nobody except any Parker employee with master keys to the whole place. Right now, we're sitting ducks. We've got to get someplace safe and lay low while we find out where Ted has gone. Someone at CBC might be able tell us," I suggest.

"What can we do?" Kate wonders.

Using my laptop, I check the train schedule for Ottawa and find that the next train goes at 11:01 a.m. Friday. I look up the number for the Westside Motel, pick up her phone and call, making a reservation for tonight.

"I'm going to drop you at the motel and leave you to take the train tomorrow. I'll drive to Ottawa, but because I'll be alone in the car, they probably won't bother with me. You are the loose end they are worrying about."

We pack a few things in the suitcases. I take my biggest bag but put in only a change of underwear and a week's worth of pills. I set an interval timer to turn the lights on at night and off in the daytime. We hurry out to the car and drive out Main Street to the Westside Motel.

I park in front and we go in with just my big suitcase and the phones. Kate has a few 'buts' when I leave her suitcase in the car but quietens down when I put my finger to my lips. When we get to the room, I set Kate's buggy phone on the desk, suitably plugged in to the charger. I explain the plan and she gulps but agrees to it.

I go out and drive to the rear of the motel. I park near the back door near the kitchen. I pop the trunk but hold the lid down to a position where I can lift it up easily.

When I return to the room, I help Kate work herself into a scrunched-up ball in my big suitcase. I zipper her in and trundle her past the motel's kitchen enroute to the car. I get some funny looks, but no one tries to stop me.

It is no small feat lifting the suitcase into the car, but I manage it. I close the car trunk after unzipping the 'Kate' trunk so that she can stretch out a little and breathe okay. I head for Highway 15, the shortest route to Ottawa.

Ten minutes later, when we come to Lakeview Road about three kilometers from the intersection of 401 and 15, I turn left and drive to Geoffrey's home. Geoffrey taught at the Alternative School in Linden and we are good friends. When I park on the grass at the end of his long driveway, I open the trunk and help Kate out.

The lot is a couple of acres in size and our car is well-hidden from the little traffic that goes by on Lakeview Road. We approach the front door and I push the button that sits below a hand-printed sign that says 'Bell' with a down-pointing arrow.

"Hi, Geoffrey," I say when he opens the door. "This is Kate. We wonder if you can put us up for a couple of nights."

Like me, he is retired. Also like me, he is extremely adaptable, having dealt with students who want to be anywhere but in school. He doesn't even blink.

"Come in," he says. "I am just thinking of preparing some supper. Would you care to join me, or have you eaten already?"

He is tall and thin, probably six foot two. He has a smile permanently plastered on his face, probably etched in place by the years of being amused by the antics of his students.

We sit around that evening and chat about old times. I don't say a word about Kate's situation other than that she arrived in Canada about fourteen months ago and is looking for contract work these days. I feel it is better not to put Geoffrey in an awkward position should some gangsters happen to find us.

His home is a modern, two-storey building. It has balconies on the second floor and a large, covered deck out back where he sits and watches the wildlife enjoy the waters of the Reesor. His garage is jammed full of watercraft, a canoe, two kayaks and an inflatable dinghy with a small outboard motor. When he shows us the garage on our tour of the house, we understand why his car is parked outside.

At bedtime, Geoffrey thoughtfully asks "One bedroom or two?"

We both say "Two."

I follow up with the revelation that I am merely an acting chauffeur. Kate adds "We bumped into each other just last Sunday. Good old Bill is helping me get some contract work."

Friday turns out to be sunny although a little cool. After breakfast I tell Geoffrey that on second thought we are going to push on, rather than impose on him for a second day.

"There's a chance for something in Rideau Falls so we'll head there this morning."

We say our "Many thanks" and "Goodbyes" and climb back in the car. I am sure that no one from Parker will be looking for us in this area. Kate sits in the front passenger seat and we discuss our plans in more detail.

"I think we should lay low for at least a week," I say. "I'm sure as hell not going to Ottawa or back to Linden. Do you have any suggestions?"

Kate purses her lips and then shakes her head.

"It's your territory. I don't have the slightest idea. Did you want to hole up in that place you mention to Geoffrey? I think you said Rideau Falls," she recalls.

"Well," I say, "the trouble with a small place like that is that you would shine like a beacon. There are very few black people there and the simplest inquiry will reveal your whereabouts. I have a summer cottage on an island about 40 kilometers from here. We can stay there and be sure that no one will see us as it is deserted at this time of year. The cottages are not winterized so everyone is away in their winter home."

"Wouldn't it be too cold?" asks Kate. "You say it's a summer cottage. Mid-November is hardly summer. Last winter in Toronto it was so cold I nearly froze to death just waiting for a subway," she claims.

"It would certainly be difficult," I admit. "We would need a week's supply of food and drinking water. The only electricity is from solar panels. The stove runs on propane and the warmest building is a sleeping cabin three hundred yards from the main cottage. It is 170 square feet in size with a double bed and an air-tight woodstove. And, of course, we'd have to drive to a manually-operated ferry to transport us and the car onto the island."

"It sounds lovely," says Kate. "Are there polar bears too?"

"You laugh," I say. "There are beaver there, the occasional deer or fox and one summer we actually heard a wolf call. No mosquitoes in November though."

Kate finally agrees that roughing it at the cottage would be preferable to being caught by Kirkman and dealt with in the same mysterious manner as with Ted Simmons.

I point out that it would give us a chance to plan our next steps with no interruptions. As a result, we pull into a grocery store in Eaton and I ask Kate to stay in the car while I pick up enough food to keep us going for a week. Luckily, they have the five litre bottles of drinking water, so I take two lighter bottles rather than a ten-litre one.

We drive through the back roads until we reach the isthmus, the point of land where the car ferry can be used to get us on the island. To my dismay, the ferry has been taken out of the water and is sitting immobile, smack in the middle of the relatively narrow road. I carefully back up until we find a place wide enough for me to turn the car around.

"That's right, I remember now. They take the ferry out of the water for the winter," I say.

"What's plan B?" asks Kate.

"Don't be funny," I grouse. "All we need is a canoe and we can easily paddle there. We can walk there if we can get across here at the isthmus, but that will involve carrying those boxes of food three miles and I don't think that will work. There's another road that goes part way up the peninsula between Clear Lake and ours. All we need is a canoe," I repeat. "Maybe we can borrow one."

I drive back out Isthmus Road and switch to the dirt road heading out the peninsula. The road goes up and down a few steep and bumpy hills. Eventually we stop at a deserted cottage all boarded up for the winter.

"I paddled out from my cottage to this place in December one year," I say. "It was snowing, but there was no ice on the lake. We will have to be careful not to tip because the water is about one degree above freezing and you won't last awfully long in water that cold."

"I won't last even that long," says Kate. "I can't swim."

"Hang on and I'll see if there's a boat we can borrow," I say.

I walk around the property, checking the outbuildings. Everything is locked up tightly.

I go back and report.

"There are about five more cottages along the peninsula beyond here. I expect there are some foot paths. No road though. Do you want to wait in the car while I see if I can find a boat or canoe or do you want to hike with me through the woods?"

"I'll stay in the car," Kate decides. "If you're not back by dark, what should I do?"

"I'll leave you one set of the keys," I say. "If I'm not back by dark, go to the police and report another missing man."

I am joking, but she takes me seriously.

"Okay," she says. "Do you want a banana before you go?"

"Good idea," I agree as we haven't eaten since we left Geoffrey's home.

We sit in the car and enjoy a last meal together.

"It's certainly quiet here," says Kate.

"Yes. It will be good to be able to just sit and think things through with no worries," I reply.

I know there is a good chance I can find a boat or a canoe. I leave both a boat and two canoes outside all winter. They are upside down. Water and snow don't affect them.

Since the road ends at this property, the cottagers who live further out the peninsula probably park a car at a marina and finish the trip by boat. As a result, the paths through the woods are not used much.

At this cottage, the peninsula is quite narrow. It broadens out as I make my way along. The woods are so thick I can't see the lakes on either side through the trees. The path splits left and right about 200 yards in and I choose to go to the right. I know enough to stay on the path. A tree has fallen and blocks my way, but I climb over the trunk easily.

Eventually, I come to a steep rise and from the top I spot a clearing and a cottage by the shore of the lake. The terrain is rough, rocky in places, so I walk carefully to the lake front.

Sure enough, they have left a canoe upside down on the grass beside a dock. Two paddles are carefully stowed under it. Unfortunately, there are no life jackets. I figure the risk of tipping is slight. Kate will sit on the floor. I'll pack the supplies around her and warn her to be still.

I launch the canoe and paddle back to the cottage to Kate and the car. To my dismay, the car, with all my supplies, is gone.

'Damn that woman,' I say to myself. 'What in the world is she thinking? Surely she knows I'll be stranded here.'

I pull the canoe out of the water, invert it beside the cottage and put the paddles under it. I walk to where the car was parked only thirty minutes earlier. I examine the dusty roadway and see where she has turned the car around. To my additional dismay, I see the tire tracks of a second vehicle. Wide tires. A man's footprint is near where the driver's side front door of my car would have been.

Is that my shoe size? I compare my left shoe to the indentation in the road. No! My shoe fits well inside it. 'My God,' I realize, 'they've found us, and they have taken her.'

I walk to the cottage and sit on the front steps while I try to determine what to do next.

'How could they have found us?' I wonder. 'I bet that they put a bug on my car. They knew where we were the whole time,' I conclude.

Eventually, I realize that it will do no good to sit there waiting for night to descend while considering every possibility. I decide to walk and think at the same time. I head for the dusty road and up the first hill.

It is a good five miles before I reach Highway 15 and darker than a tomb when I get there. I am near Roxboro. I walk the extra five hundred yards to where a County Road crosses 15 and stand at the side under a bright light with my thumb out, hoping for a ride. Three cars go by, but the fourth has a young man driving and he pulls over.

"Where are you headed?" he asks.

"Ironside," I say.

"Hop in," he tells me, and I do, rather slowly, every muscle aching.

He drops me at the Ironside Country Inn where I book a room and have an excellent supper.

'At least, this is better than a freezing cottage,' I decide.

Chapter 8

Since there is no public transport between Ironside and Linden, I call on Geoffrey Saturday morning and he kindly drives out and retrieves me. When we get near Linden, I say "What the heck, you might as well take me to my apartment. I'll tidy up there and then rent a car if I need one."

He has discerned that Kate has stolen my car and scooted off to places unknown and he simply shakes his head, thinking but not saying anything about old men and their dreams.

He drops me at the front door. He declines an offer to come in and help me finish my bottle of Scotch, and off he goes.

I go into the front vestibule, use my fob to open the door to the front lounge and head to the elevator. I slip on my mask when another tenant comes out of the elevator. A minute later I am safely in my apartment where I unplug my tricky light timer.

I make a coffee and review the week since Kate dropped into my life. Certainly, her presence helped me get organized in Linden. I wonder when I would have given up on the Bayshore Inn and found an apartment had she not bounced into my booth in the restaurant with her wild tale of intrigue. At least, I'm settled in a nice apartment.

Remembering the Alexa that came with the apartment, I ask "Alexa, what date is it?"

Her matter-of-fact voice responds: "It is Saturday, November the fourteenth, twenty twenty."

After some serious consideration, I realize that Parker doesn't care about me. They just want to silence the CBC investigators. Since both Ted and Kate are now under their control, they probably aren't worrying about me. A quick review of my rent application form will reveal that I am 88 years old and if they bother to check, my Facebook page will show that they have nothing to fear from a great-grandfather who writes mystery stories for 10-year-olds.

I feel somewhat relieved knowing that they will not bother with me and then realize that their negligence will leave me free to investigate provided I keep my head down and don't try to interview Kirkman myself.

I start planning my investigation by listing everything I know about Parker and the lucrative criminal activity they might be pursuing.

Unfortunately, it is a short list. All I know about Parker is that they own, manage, and rent out apartments. There are other companies with the Parker name, and I presume that they are subsidiaries. My knowledge of lucrative criminal activity is limited to the mystery novels I read, most of which throw in something criminal to provide a setting for a complicated murder plot. Kate had mentioned girls from Eastern Europe and drugs from Mexico.

With the border closed due to the covid-19 pandemic, I will concentrate on on-going activities, such as, for example, prostitution or local drug sales. I won't be able to find out how they are importing drugs, but I can possibly find a connection to sexual services they provide locally.

Using the Internet, I find a list of Linden massage parlours. These are semi-legal institutions that front for prostitutes under the guise of offering full body massages. One called "High Society" offers escorts and erotic massages. They even offer 'GFE', a term I don't know. Google tells me it means "Girl Friend Experience". The lady will pretend that she's my girl friend as she escorts me to a restaurant meal or gives me an erotic massage. She might even kiss me. I bet they'll rescind that offer when they see that the client is a slobbering octogenarian.

I somehow don't think that I can survive an erotic massage at my age and move on to click on "Attendants". There I find brief descriptions of fifteen ladies, all in their twenties, who will be an escort or provide massage services. They are pictured wearing very scanty outfits. More importantly, the brief description indicates that they are all healthy

Canadian girls; only one is a European-Canadian. This is not the website of sex slaves illegally imported from Eastern Europe.

To confirm my analysis, I see that they do not work on Sundays, so clearly these people are not people who consort with gangsters.

I glance at my watch and discover that it is supper time, so I take a break and have a salmon salad sandwich and a glass of milk. I find a bag of Smarties hiding behind a package of Quick Quaker Oats and munch on a few of them as dessert.

The Saturday night TV is not particularly inspiring so I shuffle off to bed at 9:15 with the idea that perhaps I can come up with a plan tomorrow to rescue Ted, who I've never met, and Kate, who has been kidnapped along with my car.

I wake up bright and early, shower, have breakfast, and am ready to continue my research by 8:15.

I find Parker quite easily. Their website details the names of their executives. It turns out that Kirkman isn't the owner or the general manager. Ted has that wrong. Kirkman oversees Information Technology, my old profession; he's a computer guy.

A little more research reveals that the company has indeed been around a long time and their Chairman is a generous philanthropist, having donated millions to hospitals in Linden. No wonder the police consider the work of Ted and Kate amateurish. Two minutes of research shows that the Parker companies are above reproach.

Kirkman himself is a little unusual. It seems he enjoys considerable wealth from selling his software company at the height of the dot com boom, just before the turn of the century. I feel a kinship because I am enjoying the good life with the bucks I made from the sale of my software company at that time.

In an interview with a Linden reporter, Kirkman implies that he's working with Parker despite not needing the pay as it provides a challenge for him to apply his computer knowledge to a field that has not been automated.

In a recent speech he names three people who influence him: Elon Musk of Tesla fame, Jim Pattison, the billionaire owner of groceries in Western Canada and Larry Page, one of the founders of Google.

I could hardly disagree with his choice of mentors. Musk is promoting doing away with silos. With that he means that all employees of Tesla companies are to work together with the common goal of making Tesla profitable. He doesn't want a space division and a car division although that's what he has now. Maybe that's why he used his space company to send one of his cars to orbit Mars.

In addition to owning and managing apartment buildings, Parker is also an Internet provider. They have a string of grocery supermarkets, and food delivery trucks to move food from wholesalers to retailers. They also own Parker Moving and Storage. Since the start of the covid pandemic, they provide a grocery with basic food supplies in their apartment buildings so that their tenants do not need to venture outside. Everything pushes the Parker brand and I presume that all the employees consider themselves to be part of the Parker family.

Pattison is well-known for his selection of good people to manage his companies and his emphasis on knowing his customers. He is the epitome of the person who says the customer is always right. In Burnaby where I used to shop, his grocery store manager is on the floor helping customers for at least an hour each day. Since the onset of the covid pandemic, his stores provide free home delivery of grocery orders placed online.

The Pattison name appears on many billboards in every province in Canada. It also appears on plaques on hospital wings in Vancouver. He is one of the major contributors to the replacement for St. Paul's Hospital, a mainstay of downtown Vancouver.

Page made his name with the Google search engine. The key to his success is in management of what they call 'big data', detailed information on everything. His mapping service has cars with roof cameras taking a photo of every address on every street in America initially and by now, probably every street in the world.

Zuckerberg of Facebook is doing the same sort of thing with big data. Google and Facebook are developing so-called artificial intelligence programs (A.I.) that can learn. That is, the computer system using A.I. can make better decisions than people can because they analyze vast quantities of data more rapidly.

As I think about the recent advances in computer applications, I begin to get a glimmer of what Kirkman might be doing at Parker. He provides a free Alexa device with the apartment. With high-speed Wi-Fi in every building, carefully integrated with building systems, he can do a lot more than simply keep the temperature under control. If he has access to every word that is spoken in every apartment and his computers can convert speech to text and analyse what his tenants are saying, he may be able to build a system that knows what every tenant is planning, almost determining what he is thinking.

I wonder if he knows that Canadian privacy laws find this invasion of privacy totally illegal. In Canada, you must give explicit permission to anyone who is going to collect personal, private information about you.

I remember that there are twelve pages in the lease agreement that I initialled as the lady signing me up explained each paragraph of the long, boring agreement.

'Oh-oh,' I think, 'maybe I'd better read that agreement.'

I go to my office area where I keep important documents in a filing cabinet. The lease agreement is there. It doesn't take long to find that on page 10 I gave up all privacy rights.

So, I conclude, they aren't doing anything illegal. Why then did they capture Kate and Ted and steal my car? Why did they leave me on a remote road five miles from the highway?

I laugh to myself thinking 'I need my ten-year-old detective, 'Brains' Cashman, of my earlier mystery novels to help.'

Chapter 9

For the next three days I research artificial intelligence and big data. It is fun to be thinking and reading about computer-related information again. It has been some twenty years since my last assignment as a computer guy. The technology has progressed at a very rapid pace and the programs I wrote then would be laughed at today.

A search of neural networks and A.I. brings up an Amazon program 'Sagemaker'. They claim that it is 'a system for machine learning for every developer and data scientist'. Under the pricing tab they promise: 'You pay only for the individual services you need for as long as you use them without requiring long-term contracts or complex licensing'.

Although this is irrelevant, I am happy to see that Amazon put the word 'only' in the correct place in that sentence. I've been really annoyed with a TV ad that says: 'Only pay for what you need'. That ad got me talking to the TV set, a worrisome problem not restricted to old age. I would say "It's pay for only what you need, not only pay for what you need, dammit."

In any case, it looks as though anyone with some computer savvy can build an application that takes text from Facebook, voice to text, or any similar system and develop its own answers on how to use that data.

When google finds an entry with 213 questions and answers related to Neural Networks and Artificial Intelligence, I know I have it made. Unfortunately, the very first question and answer makes me realize I'm way over my head.

Question: What do parameters p, q and r represent when training anfis? (I find out that anfis is 'adaptive neuro fuzzy inference system'.)

Answer: p, q and r are the consequent parameters in the fuzzy inference system first order sugeno model.

The next question has to do with grid partitioning.

At this point I give up. If Parker is into neural networks and big data, they're welcome to it. If they gain a competitive advantage over others in the business of managing apartment buildings, the more power to them. I wish them well.

I turn to something more mundane. I have a request from BC for an album of photos of friends of one of my family members. The album is carefully filed on a bookshelf, so I find it, stow it in a padded envelope that I address and stamp suitably, and take it down to the vestibule at the back door of the apartment building. There, a Canada Post installation has a slot in the wall for letters to be mailed.

However, the slot is intended for normal letters, not padded envelopes. My carefully prepared padded envelope won't go through the slot. 'Oh well,' I think, 'it's only a short walk to a standard post office box on the corner,' so I step out the back door and head for the box. It is chilly and I don't have my jacket. I move rather quickly along the sidewalk beside the parking lot.

'That's funny,' I think as I pass my car sitting in parking spot #4. 'I don't remember parking the car nose in. I usually back into the slot.'

It finally strikes me that I'm looking at my stolen car sitting there, back in its usual spot, although facing in instead of facing out. I check the door; it is locked. A glance inside shows nothing unusual. I don't have my car key with me, so I hurry on to mail my envelope and return via the front door.

Upstairs, I retrieve my spare car key. I hope that Kate has left the one I'd given her in the car. I go back down, open the car, and find my other set of keys sitting on the driver's seat. I pop the trunk. My week's worth of food for the aborted stay at the cottage is sitting in the boxes from the grocery in Eaton.

I take three more trips up and down the elevator and refill my cupboard. I leave the two five-litre bottles of water in the trunk along with my big suitcase but make a mental note to get them out before the below-zero weather arrives.

I am pleased to get the car back, but I am no further ahead in solving the mysteries that Kate and Ted have created with their intrepid investigation of Mr. Kirkman.

I decide to see if Ted is in the Canada411 directory in Toronto. A quick search reveals seven people named T. Simmons, one Tanya Simmons and fifteen E. Simmons. However, I realize that I can hardly call them in turn and ask them "Is your name Ted and are you working under contract for the CBC?" Even if I find the Ted I want, there's no way he'll answer honestly.

There are two Ngobanis in Toronto, one name Mercy and the other with the initial 'T'. It is another dead end.

In desperation, I turn on the TV to learn that Trump is continuing to stonewall attempts at transition to Biden's team. He's made Rudy Giuliani his lawyer to lead the many lawsuits that are being filed to try to overturn the results of the election. So far, 24 of the 25 lawsuits are thrown out. Someone claims that Rudy wants $20,000 per day for his services. The Trump campaign has paid three million dollars to request a recount in Michigan, so I guess a mere $20,000 a day won't be a problem.

More seriously, the covid pandemic is running wild in the States. They are averaging 150,000 new cases every day, 174,000 yesterday. Daily deaths blamed on covid are over 1700. 250,000 Americans have died so far.

In Ontario, we are getting more than 1000 new cases a day and the Premier is threatening a lockdown in Toronto. In Linden, our number of active cases has tripled from six to eighteen, still a manageable number.

In the light of these serious situations, my concerns over the past ten days' adventure seem rather trivial. I guess that Kate has told her captors that I am not part of the investigation and they left my car at my building hoping that I would simply forgive and forget. They don't expect me to raise a fuss after whatever Kate told them under duress.

Knowing that everything I say on the phone is recorded by Alexa and converted to big data by the Parker systems, I decide to phone from the car. The next stage of this investigation will be done more professionally. I reject the idea of contacting the Linden police. If Parker people are doing things legally, at least on the surface, any discussion with the local police force will get me nowhere. It is time to call in the best.

I dial the number from the website and try to marshal my thoughts so that I can explain what I need succinctly. I know that the person I am calling is a busy man. I want the best. I know I must say enough to catch his interest, but I don't want to give away the whole game just yet.

A receptionist answers.

"First Investigators. How can I help you?"

I clear my throat and say: "I'd like to speak with Mr. Laurier, please."

Laurier is the President. My experience is that it's best to start at the top.

"I'm sorry. Mr. Laurier is not in. Would you like to speak with his secretary, Miss Winston? Perhaps she can arrange to have you speak with him or someone else," she offers.

"That would be fine," I say.

"I'll transfer your call to Miss Winston then."

"Thank you," I reply.

Music cuts in for about ten seconds and then a woman speaks.

"This is Margaret Winston. How may I help you?"

'Aha', I think. 'She knows the difference between 'can' and 'may'. She can probably help'.

"Miss Winston, this is Bill Jenkins. I'm calling from Linden. I see from your website that you have offices in several cities, but I don't think you have one in Linden. Is that right?"

"That's right, Mr. Jenkins. We handle the smaller cities out of our offices here in Ottawa."

"I ask for Mr. Laurier because I find that working with the person in charge saves a lot of time. Usually, the President of a company knows best how to handle a difficult situation. I don't know Mr. Laurier, haven't met him, and I understand he is out of the office now. When do you expect him to be available?"

"You are right, Mr. Jenkins, in thinking that Mr. Laurier is our most experienced investigator. However, we have 150 investigators and support people with an average experience of twelve years in this field. I'm sure we can find someone who can help you today. Mr. Laurier will not be back for a couple of weeks. What sort of investigation do you have in mind?"

"It's a missing person case. Two missing people actually."

"Is it a couple who is missing? We do have people who specialize in domestic problems."

"No. It's a little more complicated than that. I think it will involve computer specialists who are up on the latest technology as well as some who are good at surveillance."

"I think you need to speak with Jack Moretti, our Managing Partner who is actively engaged in the field. He will know whom to assign as a suitable investigator for you. If you can hold for a moment, I'll see if he is available. Okay?" she asks.

"Sure," I agree.

I am on hold for a couple of minutes and then a deep voice says, "Moretti here."

"Hello, Mr. Moretti, this is Bill Jenkins. Miss Winston believes that you can help me."

"Yes, Mr. Jenkins. I understand you may need someone expert in computers. Many of our people are right up to date on the technology. How do the missing persons fit in?" he asks.

Miss Winston has clearly briefed him rather quickly.

"I met a young woman who is supposedly investigating a Linden company for a CBC project. Her partner disappeared. He didn't show up at a rendezvous. She went ahead with an interview, got scared, left suddenly, found me, and a week later she disappeared too. The person she was meeting is a computer guy. That's where the computers come in. I'm a professional writer so I've written the situation up."

"It sounds rather complicated," Moretti comments. "Can you send me your report on it?"

"Yes," I assure him. "I don't trust the Internet. I'll print it and courier it to you. You can let me know next week as to whether or not you think your company can help."

"I'll look forward to reading your report," he replies.

I thank him and sign off.

I back the car out of slot #4, turn it around and back it in again, facing out, the way it should be.

I spend the rest of the day finalizing the summary of the key events and any relevant thoughts I have. I print the report and send it off to First Investigators along with a complete "Assignment Form" from their website. At last, I can relax. The problem will soon be out of my hands.

Chapter 10

On Monday at 4 pm I get the call from First Investigators. Moretti is on speaker phone with a couple of his colleagues listening in.

"I hope you don't mind, but it's better if everyone hears what you have to say first-hand," he says.

"No. It's fine," I reply.

"First of all, Mr. Jenkins, we know that you are a writer of fiction. We've checked out a few of the books you mention. We just want to be sure that what you have sent us is all true. You haven't exaggerated any of this report, have you?"

I am taken aback. Surely missing people is not a subject to be taken lightly.

"Those are the facts as I know them," I assure him. "Of course, Kate may have been lying to me. I must admit to being rather naïve. I tend to believe what people tell me, no matter how unusual it seems to be."

"Well, before we suggest a plan of action with a cost estimate for you to consider, do you mind if we try to clarify a couple of points?"

"Not at all," I say.

"We are wondering if you checked with the CBC about Kate's statement that she is working for them," he starts.

"I did check with the CBC on the Wednesday morning after I couldn't get any information from Parker's rental office. The CBC has no record of her because she is a contractor. I didn't know her partner's name at that time," I confirm.

"And after that, when Ted is missing, did you contact CBC?" he asks.

"No. Kate told me that the police spoke with the CBC."

"We did a preliminary check on Edward Simmons," says Moretti. "We suspect that if Kate's contractor actually exists, 'Ted Simmons' is not his real name. We're not sure that Kate has a partner, let alone that his name is Ted Simmons."

"You mean that Kate reported to the police that a non-existing person is missing?" I ask.

"It's possible," says Moretti. "Another question we have is related to Kate's disappearance. Are you convinced that your car is bugged? Have you checked it and found any sort of tracking device?"

"No. I didn't think of that," I admit.

"Kate could very well have simply phoned someone to get her, either when you left her to get the groceries or when you left her to find the canoe. She could have told them where to find her and have them come. They may have been following you from Eaton until you turned down the road to the peninsula. If they were that close, they could easily have come while you are looking for a canoe," he pointed out.

"Well," I say. "Those points cast a vastly different light on what has happened. It's just that I wonder why anyone would do all that, go to those lengths. Is it a practical joke on me, do you think?"

"We cannot tell without a deeper investigation. Unless you think that there is some alternate explanation of what seems to be a harmless prank that someone is playing on you, I'd suggest you save your money. Based on our extensive investigation experience and the fact that Parker has a sterling reputation, we recommend that you forget about it. Someday, someone may laughingly tell you about it and why they enjoyed making you traipse around following their clues. I'm afraid there's nothing criminal here," he states.

"Thank you, Mr. Moretti," I say. "Please send me an invoice for your time and trouble. I appreciate getting this wise advice from professional investigators," I add.

"There is no charge for this service," says Moretti. "We hope you will speak well of us when you publish your novel."

"You can be sure of that," I say. "Thank all your staff members for handling this so well."

I click off my phone and say to Alexa: "Alexa, take that!"

She replies: "I'm sorry, I do not know that."

Then I begin to worry. Out loud I ask myself "Did I make her up? Am I losing my mind?"

Alexa doesn't answer.

Chapter 11

All Monday evening and at least until noon on Tuesday, I stew and worry about who would have played such a prank on me. At last, I shake it off and conclude that a prank is simply one possible explanation of the events. Perhaps First Investigators simply don't want to take on the project and use the prank idea to kill it.

While I am worrying about the so-called prank, our neighbours to the south breathe a sigh of relief when the U.S. Government approves the transition to the presidency of Biden.

I consider many questions.

Is Kate working for a rival company and doing industrial espionage? Is she trying to find out what makes Parker so profitable?

Is Kate working for a government agency trying to find out if Parker is violating tax or privacy laws?

Does Ted Simmons exist? Is his name a fake one?

Why would Kate want to be rescued from my plan to spend a week at my remote cottage? Perhaps she is working against a deadline and a week away from the action would cramp her efforts.

I go back to the first time I met Kate and examine the situation from an unbiased point of view. Did she happen to pick me at random or was I targeted? Even before that, how reasonable is her explanation about leaving the meeting with Kirkman. She claims that she walks out of his building and catches a cab immediately. My experience with Linden cabs is that I order them in advance. They don't cruise the streets hoping to be flagged down the way they are in New York City. As well, Kate is supposedly a junior member of the CBC team, yet she goes ahead with the meeting when her boss doesn't arrive.

The more I analyze it, the more I feel that the meeting with me is planned and staged so that I will become her protector. Is the plan to select someone at random or does it aim at me to be her protector? I conclude that I am target.

Another realization strikes me as significant. Her seeming confusion about who I am and her baseless claim that she doesn't recognize the titles of my mystery-adventure stories is a bit of a clincher.

If her claim about arriving in Canada in September 2019 is true, she likely has missed the flurry of news reports about my latest story, but, of course, there is no proof that she has really lived in Africa. All in all, the initial meetings in the restaurant and hotel room have an unrealistic air to them.

I conclude that I have been chosen for the role of protector. When Kate thinks she has blown the contact with me and moves out of her apartment on Monday morning, I find it interesting that she went to the Bayshore Inn restaurant, probably hoping that I am still registered or will return to the scene of the crime.

I move on in my analysis. If this isn't a prank, why would anyone want to get me involved in the Parker situation? The obvious answer is that someone wants to use my mystery-solving skills and ability to explain complex situations in clear, concise, written reports that often go viral. Modestly, I must agree with myself.

The very act of abandoning me the way she did at Clear Lake is intended to whet my curiosity and it succeeded. It isn't a prank! It is an indirect way of asking for my help and I accept that I'm the kind of guy who accepts a challenge.

Now that I know that First Investigators has fallen for the prank hoax, I realize that I am really on my own. I can't go back to them and point out their flaws. I can't go to the police with a 'missing persons' report. I must do this on my own using unconventional methods.

In the meantime, our American friends are readying for their Thanksgiving holiday that will begin on Thursday, the 26th. The Health Authorities are pleading with everyone to stay at home. "Do not travel," they say as the number of cases of covid-19 reach 194,000 in one day and the number of deaths exceed 2,000. Sadly, although the number of air travellers is down this year when compared to the number in 2019, there are still millions who ignore the warnings.

Returning to my issue of what to do about Kate, I realize that my foremost need is to hire some staff members. I am sure that Kate is keeping tabs on me while trying to avoid being seen. I need people to flush her out.

I decide to put an ad in the paper, on Kijiji, and on Craigslist asking for people to work on a survey of discriminatory policies and practices against black and brown people in businesses in Linden. I don't specify the skin colour that interviewers should have because such a statement would not be acceptable in an advertisement, but I certainly can choose people from the black and brown communities without being too obvious about it.

By Friday, the 27th, I have seven interviewers. Three are married women, two men are students at Champlain University, and two are men laid off due to the covid pandemic. They are all dark brown or truly African black. I arrange a one-month lease of an abandoned restaurant, use the tables and chairs left by the previous tenants, and provide a cell phone for each person.

My questionnaire asks a business owner how many staff members he has and how many of them are in a visible minority, i.e., black, brown, Asian, native Indians etc. For apartment rental businesses, the questionnaire seems to reveal their discriminatory practices and it encourages them to brag that they rent to visible minorities.

After I have all the paperwork ready on November 29th I relax and watch a little TV. Trump has gotten nowhere with his various lawsuits, but he did rouse his followers with his complaints that the election has been rigged and stolen from him. So many Republicans believe him, he raises 250 million dollars for his Political Action Committee. Clearly, Biden is going to be the President on January 20th, but it is not at all clear which party will control the Senate.

Because they both have less than 50% of the vote, two Republican Senators in Georgia will defend their seats in a runoff to be held January 5th, just a month from now. The Republicans have 50 senate seats and need only one senate victory to retain control. Under senate rules, the Vice-President casts the deciding vote in a tie and the Vice-President will be Kamala Harris, a Democrat.

With the covid restrictions and so many people working from home, I don't think it makes any sense to try to interview a lot of people in person. Somehow, I want Parker to reveal if Kate is one of their tenants. It is a little tricky because I don't want my interviewers to know that they are looking for Kate. Questions involve short term rentals, whether deposits are collected and that sort of thing, always with a little explanation of why they are trying to ensure that new Canadians are being treated fairly.

Parker has a lot of apartments in town, so on Monday I assign a few to each interviewer. They are to go in person to the building, ask about renting an apartment, and record how they are treated.

By Friday, I have enough data, so I give everyone a bonus and thank them for their work. I am confident that Kate is living in one of the Parker high rise buildings on Mackenzie Street or one of the smaller buildings on Fisher. I phone each building to talk to the building superintendent, but no one admits to having anyone named Ngobani there.

Trump held a rally in Georgia tonight. Thousands of his supporters, very few of whom are wearing masks stand side by side and shout slogans at Trump. I wonder how many of them will die from covid-19 from attending the rally. Daily death totals exceed 2,500, over 100,000 people are hospitalized, and 250,000 are testing positive test for covid-19 every day.

I realize that with her living in a Parker building, Kate can get food right there. She doesn't have any real need to leave the place. Then again, if she is on a mission, she'll be spinning her wheels while she stays out of sight. If she is monitoring me, as I suspect, maybe I can spot her. To set that up, I walk to the library and take out a book.

I don't spot her following me, so I continue my walk along Turnbull Street to Norton and then down Mackenzie to Rosen. Then I wander over to Main Street, do a little window shopping, stop in for a coffee and proceed home. That doesn't work.

Tonight's TV news reports that Rudy Giuliani is in the hospital with covid-19. I fear for him. He's an old guy in his 70's.

I am always friendly with the homeless people and give them a toonie each time I stop and chat. I describe Kate and ask if anyone has seen her. I claim that she might be homeless and here in Linden. I offer a twenty if anyone can spot her.

Finally, it works. Today, in the middle of a snowstorm, my pal Chet who owns the south-east corner of King and Main, reports that Kate was in the Starbucks at Main and Wellington yesterday afternoon. She got a coffee and headed along Wellington towards Fisher Street. I hand him a twenty and thank him profusely.

Patience is one of the characteristics of a good novelist. The plot, the characters, the action, all take time to develop. As a patient novelist I station myself at the corner of Wellington and Fisher and wait for Kate to come by. I'm wearing a parka, mask, and long johns to ward off the cold. It doesn't take long.

As she passes, I say "Merry Christmas, Kate."

She looks at me, recognizes me, and is tempted to run. However, I follow my greeting with: "I'd like a True North Blend if you're going to Starbucks."

She asks: "How have you been, Bill?"

"Missing you," I admit.

We walk along to Starbucks and, thankfully, it isn't busy. We don't have to queue up outside. We sit on stools and I try to get her to open up about what is going on.

"What was that all about last month?" I ask.

"You don't want to know," she says.

"Yes, I do," I insist. "That was a mean trick to abandon me out at Clear Lake. I walked miles, much of it in the pitch dark."

"I didn't have any choice," she claims. "Those guys were on me and in the car before I could say or do anything."

"Who are they?" I ask.

"Feds," she says. "I'm under strict orders to stay put in my apartment on Fisher Street. There's some operation going on and as long as I stay out of sight and don't raise a fuss, I get a monthly payment for rent and $1,000 a week to make up for the loss of my CBC job."

"Oh, oh," I say, "I hope I haven't screwed it for you."

"No. It has nothing to do with you. When I told them who you are, they hadn't heard of you at all. They wondered why I teamed up with you. They thought that Ted was driving me around."

"Ted? Does he even exist? He's not in the Toronto phone book."

"Oh, he exists alright. That s.o.b. told me a dozen lies. His name isn't Ted, but I still think of him as Ted. His name is Rob Dunphy, and he works for C.S.I.S., the Canadian Security Intelligence Service. He got called off to Ottawa before our meeting with Kirkman and didn't bother to tell me," she says.

"Are you with C.S.I.S. too?" I ask.

"Well, in a way I am now, only because they are paying me and putting me up in that apartment. I'm not an employee or even a contractor. They just want me out of the way while they try to get the goods on Kirkman. They are paying me to lay low.

There was no CBC contract. Ted was trying something with Kirkman, but his boss pulled him off. He sent his team to get me out of the way. They paid me for 85 Front Street originally and thought I was still living there when they brought me back," she says.

"How did they find you? My plan was foolproof."

"I have no idea, but they eavesdrop on anybody they want. If it has to do with national security, they have carte blanche," she says.

"Can you join me for dinner? I want to learn more about this case."

"I'm afraid not. I have other plans for dinner almost every night. We can meet afternoons for coffee if you like, but I have obligations for dinner and evenings. I probably shouldn't have told you this much, but I owe you an explanation for disappearing."

"Do you come here for coffee every day?"

"Not every day. It's okay to come here for coffee, but I should get back now. It's nice to see you again. You don't need to worry about me. I'm fine."

She slides off the stool and heads for the door. I don't attempt to stop her. I figure I'll find her here again and maybe dig a little more out of her another time if I don't push it.

Back in my apartment, I update my report on the intrepid investigator and note that my conclusion is right. It isn't a prank!

Chapter 12

After a couple of meetings at Starbucks with Kate, I begin to prefer their coffee over my homemade Instant. Kate meets me there and gradually she lets me know how things are working out. It turns out that she's making much more money than she ever has, in part because she got Kirkman to agree to provide a free apartment for a few months in return for dropping her CBC investigation of the company. I guess she has more nerve than sense. Kirkman will be mad if he learns that there really isn't a CBC investigation. She says she hasn't told him about C.S.I.S. and she hasn't told C.S.I.S. she's getting the apartment for free.

The other thing she admits is that she works nights at High Society as an attendant. She claims she makes $100 per hour for doing a simple back rub or for providing a 'girl friend experience' date with a client.

"It's fun," she says, and I get well paid.

"Isn't it really prostitution, Kate?" I ask quietly.

"Oh no!" she exclaims. "Some of the girls provide extras, but that's always a negotiation between the girl and the client. The company isn't involved in extras. The client pays the attendant directly. The neat thing is that everybody gets a month-end bonus. They share half the company's net profit equally with all the workers at the end of the month. I get the same bonus as everyone else no matter how many hours I work. I'm making money hand over fist!"

"And do you provide extras?"

"Nope. I just let the client have a good time. Most of them don't even want a massage. The GFE is what's missing in their life and by my being cheerful, happy and a little loving, it makes them feel that they are getting what they want. Funny thing is, I'm getting enough dinner dates that my food costs are way down."

"What can you tell me about the C.S.I.S. operation? Do you keep in touch with them?" I ask.

She explains that she is totally out of the loop now.

"They deposit money in my bank account every week, $1,000 in lieu of having a job, and $1,800 every month for rent. I never see them, and I like it this way. I just hope that they have a long, long investigation."

"It certainly sounds as though you've got it made," I say. "I shouldn't have worried about you. You've landed on your feet.

I may be out of town for a while," I report. "Don't worry if you don't see me at Starbucks for a few weeks. I'm going to spend Christmas with a cousin of mine in Pembroke. I'll be back just before the New Year and will look for you then."

"Where's Pembroke?" she asks.

"It's on Highway 7 heading North on the way to Camp Petawawa or North Bay," I say. "I'll tell you all about it when I see you after Christmas."

"Have a good time," she says. "I'll probably be busy New Year's Eve. I'll look for you here in January."

"Right," I agree as we part.

I don't have a cousin in Pembroke. I just want to have a quiet time while I digest what I've learned.

When I look up Parker apartments in Canada, I find that they are in twenty cities in Ontario and one in the West. With fifteen buildings in Toronto, forty in Linden, and thirty in Ottawa, they have a sizeable portfolio. Their total annual revenue is about 50 million dollars, counting all their businesses. I can see why Canada Revenue Agency might be interested in them as they no doubt pay a good amount in income taxes, but why are they a target for C.S.I.S.?

Now that I know that Kate is okay and Ted, a.k.a. Rob Dunphy, is not missing, I can let sleeping dogs lie. Maybe I should wrap this case up and turn to 'The Case of the Jinxed Jewel'.

As radical as the idea is, I wonder if maybe I should skip this method of naming my stories and call this one 'The Case of the Missing Investigators Who Weren't Missing After All'.

I decide to sleep on it.

Chapter 13

I still have a few friends in Ottawa from the days of contract consulting at Supply and Services and Canada Post. I remember that my office at Canada Post looked out on a building housing one group of C.S.I.S. employees. We tried to avoid looking towards the C.S.I.S. building because we thought that their people were paranoid and would void our security clearance if we annoyed them by staring too much.

Some wags say that the reason not to spend the morning looking out the window is so that we'll have something to do in the afternoon.

I spend the morning checking for names and addresses of my bosses from those days. Of course, they have all retired twenty-five to thirty years ago and most of them are long since gone. I check the Ottawa Citizen obituary reports to determine if they are still in the land of the living.

Eventually I conclude that the only one left who can help me is Tom Scully. He's retired from External Affairs and is living in a Senior's residence in the Woodroffe section of Ottawa. I reach him by phone, and he is surprised to hear from me.

"It's Bill Jenkins," I tell him. "A voice from your ancient past."

"Speak up, will you," he replies. "My hearing's not too good."

After a bit of to and fro, we establish contact, and he agrees to see me.

"You'll have to wear a mask," he says. "We're not under lockdown now, but we have been a couple of times. Do you want to try for lunch? This place has a decent cafeteria, but it's pretty noisy."

"Lunch is fine," I say. "I'll pick you up and we can get some take out from a local restaurant. I don't want to mingle indoors with all the covid-19 you have in Ottawa."

"Okay," he says. "I don't get out much and it will be good to catch up on your news."

We agree that I'll be there at 11:30 so that we can pick up some food before the lunch hour rush.

I pack my big suitcase with enough clothes to last a week and make a reservation for Christmas Eve at the Byward Inn in the Byward Market area for $90 plus taxes.

Although it's only a two-hour drive to Ottawa, I leave the apartment at 7:30 a.m. as I don't want weather or any other problem to hold me up. Tom is the only contact I have. I don't want to miss this chance to get his advice.

As I suspect, the roads are clear, and I check in at the downtown hotel in plenty of time to make it out to Tom's Senior Residence on Lockhart Avenue. He is waiting at the entrance as I drive up. He walks to the car sturdily, with the help of a cane.

He opens the door before I can get out to open it for him.

"You're looking pretty good, Bill," he says.

"Clean living," I claim. "How are you doing?"

"I use the cane for balance more than anything else. Other than that, I have no complaints."

He has grown a full beard since I last saw him. I would never have recognised this distinguished senior, a former civil servant.

"I'd never have recognised you, Tom," I say. "That beard and mustache make you look so cool. You must be a hit with the ladies in your building."

"They're all too old for me," he says. "There's nobody under 70 there. Trouble is, with this covid, I don't get around much anymore."

"I don't suppose you've pitched many games recently," I say, referring to his success as a juvenile fastball pitcher in Montreal.

"Not for 50 years," he says. "My arm is gone anyway. If I were still working at Global Affairs, I wouldn't even be able to push a pen," he laughs.

We drive to a nearby restaurant, Mia's Indian Cuisine.

"Is Indian okay?" I ask.

"I'd actually prefer MacDonald's," he replies. "The spicy food doesn't agree with me."

We find one on Carling just past Riddell Avenue, order hamburgers, fries and milkshakes, and park in the huge Carlingwood parking lot.

"What brings you to contact me?" Tom queries. "It's been twenty years or maybe longer since we've even chatted."

"I want to pick your brain, of course," I reply. "I was mostly with Supply and Services. I didn't have a contract with External Affairs, the R.C.M.P. or with C.S.I.S. although I did get a certificate as a security expert when I worked for the Service Bureau. I want to find out how External Affairs ties in with C.S.I.S."

"Well, to bring you up to date, External Affairs is now Global Affairs Canada. C.S.I.S. is responsible for the security of G.A.C. personnel around the world. They aren't police and don't arrest anyone. They are Canada's spy service in terms of our spying and our counter-espionage activities that catch the spies of other countries. Many of our spies work out of our embassies as do many of the foreigners spying in Canada.

R.C.M.P. is responsible for investigation of criminal activity at every level, municipal, provincial, federal, and international. They work in conjunction with C.S.I.S. if something criminal is found and C.S.I.S. wants someone arrested."

"What kind of work did you do at External Affairs?" I ask.

"Sorry. I'm still bound by the Official Secrets Act. I can't discuss what I did or anything that is classified," Tom says.

"Fair enough. The reason I ask is that I heard that a company in Linden is being investigated by C.S.I.S. Actually, I think they are investigating the I.T. person."

"Is that at Champlain University?" Tom asks.

"No. A private company."

"I could understand investigating a university professor because they often have international contacts and sometimes their research is of interest to other countries. What kind of company is it?"

"Pretty run of the mill," I say. "They are a conglomerate. They own and rent apartments. Most of their subsidiaries are service industries supplying their tenants. I'm living in one of their apartments."

"How did you hear about C.S.I.S.?" Tom asks.

I give him a brief overview of what I've learned. He lets me describe it all in detail and doesn't interrupt with questions. I finish with "So that's why I called you."

Tom glances around the parking lot and, in an incredibly quiet voice, asks: "Is this your own car or did you get a rental?"

"It's mine."

"Is it the one you are driving when Kate disappears? The one that is stolen?"

"Yes, of course," I say, "but I didn't report the theft and it was returned in a couple of days."

"Shit," says Tom. "Every word of our conversation is undoubtedly recorded and is winging its way through their computer systems. You know, I presume, that they can convert voice to text extremely reliably. A complete report will be sitting on your handler's desk before he leaves tonight."

"I don't have a handler," I object. "I'm just a nobody that Kate happened upon when she thought she was being chased by Kirkman's people. I haven't said a word to anyone in government, let alone C.S.I.S."

"For the record, I want everyone to know that this is the first and also the last I've heard of this," says Tom in a loud clear voice. "I haven't seen you in twenty years and you call me up to chat on Christmas Eve about something ridiculous like this. Take me back to Lockhart and don't call again. I know nothing about this little mystery, and I don't wish to know anything about it," he says.

I gather that perhaps I should take him back to his senior's home, so I do. He doesn't speak again. It is only a few blocks. He doesn't wish me a "Happy Holiday" or "Happy New Year". All I hear as he stomps away is "Amateurs!"

'Where have I heard that before?' I wonder.

I drive back downtown, put the car in a parking garage, and walk to my room in the Byward Inn. I am rather distracted. Tom acted as though I am dragging him into some sort of dangerous situation. We didn't speak about anything classified and he hasn't talked about his work. What can be bothering him?

I take a couple of mini bottles of Scotch from the in-room liquor cabinet and pour myself a double. I unpack my bag and switch on the TV. Christmas music is playing on every channel, so I turn it off and have a taste of my drink. I really don't have a clue as to how to proceed. 'Should I just take a holiday for a week? After all, it is Christmas.'

I sit in the comfortable chair, put my feet up on the bed, and ponder life in general. I was born in Ottawa, lived here many years as a child and later as a computer consultant. I think about the many Ottawa friends I have lost over the years. 'I guess that's the curse of a long life,' I think.

Remembering one friend, Harry Michaels, who was a student at Champlain University with me, I pull out my phone and check to find his number. 'He lives in Kanata, I think'.

I find his entry and press the 'call' icon. Because my hearing is a little sketchy at times, I click on speaker phone.

It takes a few explanatory statements to get Harry to realize who is calling. He's a year older than I am, so 89 now. We haven't spoken since my time in Vancouver and he is surprised to hear that I am calling from downtown Ottawa.

"What brings you over here?" he asks.

"I moved to Linden after Margaret died," I say. "I came here today to chat with an old friend, Tom Scully. Do you know him? Retired from External Affairs."

"That's Global Affairs Canada now," says Harry. "I don't know him, but my son might. He retired from Global last July. I really don't know many people in government now. I've been retired almost twenty years and all my contacts are dead or forgotten."

"Tom's a good friend of mine. He used to be the best fastball pitcher in Montreal in the fifties and you may remember, Margaret's cousin was the best in Toronto in those days."

"Believe it or not, Bill, I don't remember. I'm happy enough to know it's Christmas Eve again. Merry Christmas, by the way."

"Well, same to you and many of them. I just want to say 'Hi' and wish you the best."

"My son and his wife will be here for Christmas dinner tomorrow. If you don't have anything planned, why not drop out for a short visit tomorrow afternoon. With covid, we don't see many people these days and we limit visits to an hour according to what the health experts say. If you come for 4 p.m. we'll have a glass of sherry," he promises.

He gives me the address and I say I'll be there.

I check out the next morning at 11 because I realize that there are no more contacts for me to see. I drive around Woodroffe where I grew up. The house on Deschenes was replaced with a duplex a few years ago and I haven't seen the new look. All the cottages on the waterfront are gone.

A scenic parkway now runs along beside the Ottawa river. It is sobering to see the tiny homes where my childhood friends used to live.

The dump is gone. It was a wooded area on the east side of Woodroffe Avenue north of the railway tracks. It held a million treasures for us to discover. An endless source of building materials for ten-year-old scavengers now hosts a two-storey, landscaped home. Even the railway tracks are gone.

I make my way out to Harry's in time, following the instructions from google maps. Kanata has changed from farmland to suburbia. There is no place to park near Harry's townhouse, but I find a spot one street over and walk back. Harry is his usual self, sardonic and enjoying life. He claps me on the back and nearly knocks me over.

Harry's wearing a bright red Christmas jacket, casual trousers, and new Christmas slippers that he brags about. His wife, Susan, brings a tray of hors d'oeuvres into the living room as I arrive. Harry introduces me to his son, Alec, and daughter-in-law, Sandra.

Harry and Susan were in the publishing game when they were still actively working. I'd turned to Harry for advice when I started publishing and he gave me excellent advice, starting with "Don't do it."

Alec is a bright, alert man, probably in his mid-60's since he has just retired this past summer. After the introductions, I ask him about his job at Global Affairs Canada.

"I really didn't want to retire," Alec says. "I helped develop and maintain the communication systems for our offices abroad and I was worried that the staff weren't ready and capable enough to carry on my work. They replaced me and my whole section with a corporate contract handled by Bell Canada. Some of my staff members transferred to Bell."

"I'm sure Bell Canada knows communications inside out," I say.

"Yes, of course, but they may not be used to getting a call on a Sunday afternoon with a requirement to be 10,000 miles away the next morning.

With diplomats, you must respond to outages immediately. I bet they find that aspect challenging."

We chat a bit and I learn that the diplomatic communications requirements extend well beyond having a secure telephone. He was responsible for private Internet networks, secure cell phone systems, end to end encryption and similar systems. I have a few questions and start off by assuring him I don't want to discuss anything classified.

"The reason I'm particularly interested in this whole subject," I say, "is that I came across a company based in Linden being investigated by C.S.I.S., or so the rumour that I heard goes. This company has an excellent reputation. Its main business is in real estate. It owns and manages apartment buildings which seems a far cry from spying. Did you come across C.S.I.S. in your work?"

"We worked in conjunction with them, of course, because they are expert in secure communications," Alec acknowledged. "I don't see how they would be involved unless they were, for example, targeting a tenant in an apartment rented from your Linden company. They might want to ask the company for access to an apartment for investigative work. Spies live anywhere and act like ordinary citizens so its not unreasonable that one is renting an apartment. Is this related to an Ottawa tenant?" he asks.

"I don't know," I admit. "I live in one of their apartments and the unusual thing is that their rent includes Wi-Fi provided by them and a free Alexa device. I've never had that before. I wonder if they are monitoring what I say in my apartment. Do you know if Alexa records all the time or if it is active only when I ask a question?"

"Hmm," says Alec, "I think it's always active when it is plugged in. However, the communication goes directly to Amazon via the Internet. Of course, the Wi-Fi provider could copy the sounds of your voice to its own server and convert everything to text. All that software is readily available. There are privacy concerns and listening in to a tenant's conversations is probably illegal."

"My lease agreement allows it. I suspect it's legal," I say, "but I don't go around talking to myself, at least not usually."

"Well," laughs Alec, "It may be that C.S.I.S. is investigating a rival. As you probably know, they can listen into anything that isn't encrypted, although they need a court order if they want to use the information in a trial."

"I've been reading about big data and neural networks," I say. "This artificial intelligence stuff is getting complicated. I get the idea, but the details are too much for me these days."

"Google and Facebook are certainly using A.I. and big data. Consider for a moment what the world will be like when the government and courts simply approve decisions made by artificial intelligence," says Alec. "You know that the Chinese identify all their citizens using facial recognition. In a sense, everyone there is a prisoner. They don't need prisons. Everyone there is under control. They don't dare revolt."

"That reminds me of a joke," I say. The Secretary of State tells the President 'The people are revolting' and he replies: 'They certainly are.'

Everyone laughs politely indicating that they have all heard that one before.

"I had better let you get on with your Christmas," I say. "I appreciate getting your view and comments, Alec."

Turning to Harry and the others, I make my apologies and claim that I'd better get on my way.

I certainly have enough to think about as I drive back to Linden.

'This is way above my pay grade' I think, 'considering I'm not getting paid. I'm acting like a dog chasing its own tail'.

Chapter 14

I spend the rest of Christmas alone. On Boxing Day, I phone a few friends and relatives and Skype my daughter in Switzerland. She teaches English to adults there. Most of her students are employees of drug companies. Her husband is a retired computer guy, quite a bit cleverer than I am. He could provide some suggestions for me, but I don't feel right about bringing him into this mystery. Besides, Alexa is right there, listening to everything I say.

Boxing Day is a traditional holiday in Canada. As a matter of fact, many companies shut down from some time on the 24th of December until the 2nd of January and all the staff get a paid holiday. It is unlikely that anything serious will happen until early January.

I decide it is time to catch up on my reading and start tackling the murder mysteries I have found in the Linden Public Library. As with most people, I have a few favourite authors. I have a new 'Jack Reacher' book titled 'The Sentinel' written by Lee Child and his brother, Andrew. It seems that Lee is retiring and handing the franchise off to his brother who is a good writer with a half-dozen stories published already under the name 'Andrew Grant'.

Knowing that fame requires publishing more than six books, I am pulling for Andrew to be able to produce a Reacher yarn on the same level that Lee has achieved. Having published eight stories and working on the ninth, I can understand why Andrew isn't as well-known as I am.

I settle down and become deeply involved in 'The Sentinel'. After that comes an adventure by Michael Connelly and then an old one that I've read previously, but enjoy reading again, by John LeCarre. On Monday December 28th, just as I finish breakfast, my cell rings and that ends my days of leisure.

"Merry Christmas!" says Charlie. "It's a little belated. I hope you had a good Christmas."

"Hi, Charlie. Good to hear from you. Everyone is well, I trust. There's lots of covid in Toronto. None with you and yours, I hope. Is Nancy well?"

Charlie Karai and I go back a long way. He joined the Champlain University Computing Centre when I was there, and we've kept in touch over the years. He's in his mid-70's but still doing contract work for IBM. He was the sharpest guy we had back in those days.

"We are fine, Bill. I should have called last week to wish you the best, but as usual, things got busy around Christmas."

"I've had a nice quiet time," I say. "Reading a few murder mysteries and spy thrillers. Of course, with this covid situation, I don't go out much, so I'm pleased to hear from you and hear that all is well."

"I have a bit of an unusual request to make of you, Bill. You are still in Linden, I trust. You move around so much I can never be sure."

"Oh yes, I'm here in the beautiful, snow-clad city. My desk overlooks the city, and I can see the Champlain University buildings in the distance. The apartment is quite spacious. Are you thinking of visiting? Lots of room for you and Nancy."

"Could you come here for a couple of days? I have to stay close to home, but I could certainly do with some friendly advice from my old boss," he says.

"That would be a first," I say. "What in the world could I tell you that you don't already know much better than I do? Are you planning your retirement? Perhaps you are going to start writing and need some sage advice from a world-renowned author. What is it?" I ask.

"I can't say over the phone, but it is important and urgent. I can pick you up at the train tomorrow. I need to explain a rather complicated situation to you. I want to get your ideas before next Monday because that's the deadline."

"No need to meet the train. I know where you are. It's a three-hour drive at most counting pit stops. I can be there before supper. I'm not doing anything here that can't wait," I say.

Charlie sounds relieved.

"Can you bring along enough clothes for a few days? It may not be that long, but I'm not sure at this point what all is involved."

"Sure. No problem," I assure him. "I'll see you by supper time."

"Act as though this is strictly a social visit," he says. "Nancy thinks it's just an old-guys reunion."

He adds a big "Thanks" and we hang up.

'Well,' I think, 'this sounds like the beginning of another adventure. Perhaps it is 'The Case of the Kenya Kid'. After all, Charlie's from Kenya originally.'

I sing 'On the Road Again' as I head west on 401. When I stop for gas at the Trenton Enroute station, I have a coffee and a honey doughnut to keep me going. I dig out my Willie Nelson CD when I'm back in the car and enjoy 'Stardust' and other classics as I roll along at the usual 120 km per hour.

Charlie and Nancy seem especially pleased to see me. I present them with a signed copy of 'The Case of the Hidden Hound' and they are naturally delighted with it. We have a pre-dinner drink and then sit down to Christmas leftovers.

"Did you have the whole family here for Christmas?" I ask.

"No," Nancy replies. "It's just not worth it to gamble with covid being so rampant here. Our son is in the States so he can't come anyway, and our daughter and her family agree we should wait until next year when everyone will be vaccinated."

"That's why we have so much left over," adds Charlie. "This is the third turkey meal, and we need you to help us finish it off," he says with a twinkle in his eye.

I decide that he hasn't told Nancy what this meeting is all about, so we keep the conversation on family and covid. Charlie and Nancy made the effort to fly to Vancouver a couple of years ago to say goodbye to Margaret in her nursing home. It was difficult for them to see her in her final days and I certainly appreciated their making the effort. I hope that whatever trouble Charlie is in will be something where I can help.

After dinner as Nancy starts cleaning up the dishes, Charlie suggests we head to his basement office. There he manages a team of IBM specialists all around the globe. I know his work has to do with the IBM cloud, and I certainly know I can't help him in that area.

He starts off by mentioning some of the problems that the covid-19 pandemic is creating for IBM. He points out that many companies are having difficulties with fewer staff meetings, working from home and similar matters.

"IBM is doing really well in its cloud computing. The extra advantages we have with the supercomputer 'Watson' help us immensely. The problem I want to discuss is really not an IBM one except that our philosophy is that our clients' problems are our problems too," he says.

"So, this is really a client problem. That's a relief. I was afraid you had fallen in love with a sixteen-year-old and don't know how to explain it to Nancy," I say, trying to keep it light.

"The reason I don't want to discuss this in front of Nancy is that it's a matter of the client's security. This is not to be discussed outside these four walls," he emphasizes with a serious look.

I keep quiet and let him continue.

"Covid has taken out the top I.T. management at one of our key Linden clients. Their work must go on, but they are unable to find replacements who can handle the work because their systems are very sophisticated.

They use our artificial intelligence systems to run every aspect of their business.

They need a new management team in place by next Monday, January 4th. They asked us to provide the staff and I've been tasked to find them. I've got good people for the Assistant I.T. Manager jobs, but I need a solid, experienced manager to lead the team."

"If you are looking at me, Charlie, let's be serious. I'm 88. I'm not up on artificial intelligence. They would take one look at me and switch to Amazon's cloud," I say.

"I know," says Charlie, "but I think we can pull it off. You know how to manage people; you know the basics of what the systems do; and you'll have competent people to do the technical work. I need someone who is calm, cool and collected there who can assure their President that we are handling the work."

"You must have a hundred people in Toronto alone who could manage this," I say.

"Unfortunately, no, we don't. With this covid pandemic we are stretched so thin you can't believe it. Believe me, Bill, you are not our first choice. I got the assignment on the 23rd and I've checked with every Canadian office for a senior manager. Short of going in there myself, which just isn't possible considering the project I'm managing, it turns out that I'm down to you."

"Well, I must admit I've been looking into neural networks, big data and artificial intelligence in connection with the new adventure mystery I'm writing, but that's a far cry from managing a project in the real world. One look at me and their top executives would be checking with their lawyers to cancel the IBM contract," I say.

"That's just it, Bill. What they would see is a masked manager. A toupee would take a few years off your life. I've even found a pair of gloves you can wear so nobody sees those liver marks and bruises on your hands."

"You're really serious about this," I say. "How long would this charade have to go on?"

"Just until Kirkman recovers from his covid," says Charlie.

That floors me. I don't let on I know the name, but suddenly I realize that he is talking about Parker.

"Kirkman?" I ask. "Who is Kirkman?"

"He's the I.T. executive responsible for the systems at this client's headquarters. He caught covid-19 and spread it to his three I.T. managers. They are all positive and all isolating until they get two negative tests a week apart. The earliest they'll be back is January 19th, so we need you to hold down the fort until then. After that, you'll be out quickly because there won't be a lot to turn over. It's really only a two to three-week period," Charlie points out.

"The thing is," he adds, "they don't want it known that so many of their executives are sick with covid. They are afraid that they'll lose the confidence of their customers and that competitors will try to push down the value of their holdings. That's why we have to keep this secret."

"How bad will it be if your client finds out that you've installed an ancient senior who knows nothing about this A.I. system? If they discover that I'm a has-been, they will probably throw me out and sue IBM. Wouldn't you be better to go yourself? Maybe I can hold down your job here for a couple of weeks and check with you for suitable answers to your team's questions, while you cover the Linden job. I'll even let you use my apartment," I offer.

"Won't work," says Charlie. "We are releasing an update January 4th and I'll be tied up 24/7 with problems to address. We can't postpone the update either," he adds.

"Well," I comment, "I've often suggested that I could lose 30 years by reporting my age in hexadecimal. I'm only 58, base 16."

"Now you're talking," says Charlie.

"What company is it?" I ask.

"Parker," he replies. "Their headquarters building is on Turnbull Street. That's just a couple of blocks from your apartment."

"Just like the days at Champlain University when I could walk to work, eh?"

"So, you'll do it?" Charlie asks.

"I'll think about it overnight," I say.

"Agreed," says Charlie. "Your three managers will be here at ten o'clock tomorrow morning and we can go over what we know about the company and this assignment."

"I haven't agreed yet," I say, not wanting to be seen to be that easily swayed.

Of course, I know I'll take it. Although I won't be meeting Kirkman until the assignment is all over, I figure that being on the inside and seeing what the I.T. team is doing will answer all my questions.

We go back upstairs and, reluctantly, have a scotch to seal the deal.

The next morning after breakfast, the three I.T. experts that Charlie extracted from their current projects at IBM arrive.

Barbara Allen, a 35-year-old who knows A.I. inside out, is the most senior. She can join the team because her project at a Toronto manufacturing company is not to start until mid-January. IBM figures they can handle a short delay in that project, if necessary.

Peter Rabin is only 28. He has worked for IBM for the six years since his graduation from the University of Waterloo. His area of expertise is managing big data, files that contain more than 100 megabytes of information. He will ensure that the data files in all the Parker operations are correct, complete, properly coded, filed, made accessible to other applications, and stored indefinitely in the IBM cloud for access and backup.

Josh Steubins is 32. His current assignment is to develop applications that conform to standards for a large Toronto conglomerate. Although Parker isn't large in comparison to the firm where Josh has been working, the problems are similar. He has just finished putting his latest application into production on December 1st and it is running smoothly.

All three wear masks and Charlie and I are suitably protected as well. Charlie tells them that I am an experienced manager and will be handling the liaison with other senior managers at Parker. He emphasizes that although I understood A.I. systems, I will not be doing any hands on.

"Basically, Bill is there so you guys can manage the technology without a lot of interference from the other executives at Parker. If anyone not directly under your responsibility approaches you, refer them to Bill."

Barbara asks Charlie about the A.I. system in use.

"I presume that they are using IBM Watson Knowledge Catalogue Instascan and IBM Cloud Pak. Correct?" she queries, leaving me behind in her first sentence.

"Yes," says Charlie. "Of course, they have their own code related to the data they capture, but I think we'd get into that only if a problem arises. The main thing to do for the next few weeks is to prevent any of their staff members from updating any of their production systems. We don't want to have to debug their production systems. Remember, they've been at this for a couple of years now. Their A.I. system has been trained and is meeting most of their needs."

Peter is concern about the data storage.

"Do they use the cloud exclusively or do they have local storage as well?" he asks.

"I understand that they have IBM Elastic Storage Server using IBM Spectrum Scale RAID. I don't think there is any need to worry about running out of storage anytime in the next six months. It's simple to expand storage and there is no need to re-program anything."

"What about new applications?" asks Josh.

"Find out what they are planning, but don't let them touch the production system. We're just trying to keep them afloat until their regular staff gets back."

"They must have a test version they're using for new applications," says Josh.

"Yes. You have to make sure they don't accidentally put something buggy into production."

The discussion gets into a few details, most of which sail quietly over my head. I give them my phone number and ask that they appear at the Turnbull Street headquarters at ten o'clock next Monday. I will show up at nine and get the lay of the land before their arrival. The gang leaves at noon following IBM rules that no in-person meeting should exceed two hours during the pandemic.

We have lunch and for an hour Charlie tells me what he knows of the other managers or executives at Parker. I take notes and promise to phone him if I come up with any questions before Monday. We bump elbows, the covid handshake, and I head back to Linden.

I have five days to learn all I can about Parker, their subsidiaries, their staff and especially their executives. At the same time, I need to become much more familiar with the A.I. technology so I wouldn't make a gaffe or say something that shows my lack of knowledge.

I get out my old toupee and start wearing it all day, so it won't seem too strange to be 58 again.

Chapter 15

Luckily, I still own a grey, IBM-style, business suit. Although many companies permit wearing informal attire at work, IBM still sticks to formal grey, a white shirt, and a light blue tie.

Suitably IBM'd, I take off on foot for Parker headquarters on Monday, arriving at their doorstep at 8:55. I feel that too early isn't as bad as too late, so I enter and ask the receptionist if I can see Joan Stepchild, the President of Parker. I give her one of my IBM calling cards that Charlie couriered to me on Friday.

"I'm Bill Jenkins," I say through my mask, rather unnecessarily as it is clearly written on my card.

"Please have a seat, Mr. Jenkins. She will be right with you."

When she arrives, Joan leads me back to the executive suite area, pointing out my office as we pass it. We sit in her office in a couple of easy chairs away from her rather formal desk. I am careful not to start the conversation.

I am surprised by how young she is. 'Possibly 50', I think. 'Quite young to be the President of a 50-million-dollar company'. She wears a business suit, but with a dress, not the long slacks so popular these days.

"This pandemic is getting to be awfully tiresome," she starts. "Has it affected your business much?" she asks.

"It has certainly thinned our ranks," I say, "speaking for IBM. Of course, as you know, I'm a contractor for them, not an employee, so the pandemic has increased my workload, not lessened it. Luckily, I just finished an assignment when I was called. How is Mr. Kirkman getting along? I hope he has a mild case."

"We haven't heard. The message we received suggested we leave him alone until he is better. Of course, the problem is that his whole management team is off too so that's why we called for help."

"Yes. We have three good, senior I.T. personnel assign to Parker for the duration. I asked them to come here for 10 this morning so I could meet you without any distraction. Perhaps your assistant can show me where their offices are. I want to get them running when they arrive."

"Since new faces are a rarity in our head office, I have some name tags for you to give them. I don't know how the four of you will be able to get up to speed with no real handover. What is your plan?"

"Clearly, our job is to keep things running smoothly from an I.T. perspective until your staff returns. We will put a hold on any changes to production systems and work with the programmers and other managers to try to solve any problems that come up. Our people are experienced. Barbara Allen knows the IBM A.I. systems thoroughly, so she will handle any A.I. problems. The other two are a data expert and an experienced application programmer. I'm sure we can do whatever you require."

"How about you, Bill? What's your area of expertise?"

"I'm a manager, perhaps like you. I must know everything although in fact I know nothing. I'm successful when my people are successful. I've been in the computer field for many years. I've managed as many as 75 people. As you know, my job is to make the work of my staff as effective as possible. I expect the other executives will understand it if I don't let them talk to my three managers directly. I need to keep my people on target."

"I agree with you," says Joan. "I'll have my assistant, Mary Powers, show you around. We have an executive meeting scheduled for 4 p.m. in the conference room. If you can make that you can meet the others at that time."

"Fine," I reply. "It's a pleasure to meet you," I add.

We go out and across the hall. She finds Mary who gives me the grand tour, dropping me off at Kirkman's office just before ten.

"I'm afraid George didn't get a chance to tidy up. He was out when the positive test result came, and we contacted him by phone. If you have any questions about anything, just ask me and I'll see what I can do," she offers.

I go to reception and wait until my team arrives. I show them around and leave them to handle the work on their own. I spend the rest of the day until 4 p.m. tidying up Kirkman's desk and filing his papers away. Either he'd been terribly busy, or he isn't a highly organized manager. I have the desk clear before the executive meeting at 4.

It is useful to meet the other Parker executives. I can tell that they are competent people. They receive me with grace but don't spend any time on I.T. I sit and listen for the full hour, but don't contribute anything.

The week passes well. I take a break every afternoon at about 3 and go to Starbucks for a coffee. On the Wednesday Kate shows up and we chat. I tell her that I'd heard that Kirkman has caught covid-19 but she doesn't comment on it.

On Monday, I feel rather good having survived a whole week. Then I get a call from Reception saying I have a visitor. I go to the lobby to see who it is. The man reaches out his hand to shake mine, but I ignore it.

"Sorry,' I say. "No touching during covid. How can I help you?"

"May we go to your office?" he asks. "I want to discuss some statistical reports that Mr. Kirkman usually sends me."

I lead him to my office, and he introduces himself as Rob Dunphy.

"I'm the lead scientist at Canada Artificial Intelligence Research," he claims. "We ordinarily get a weekly summary report from Mr. Kirkman and we're missing the last two reports. I learned from the receptionist that Mr. Kirkman is off sick and in isolation. I wonder if you can have someone run off the reports for me?"

I accept his statements at face value though I recognize his name. He is the 'Ted Simmons' with whom Kate has been doing the abortive CBC investigation. He is a C.S.I.S. man, not a research scientist; however, I want to determine what reports Kirkman has been supplying so I keep up the pretence.

"I'm sorry, but with George being ill, I've been assigned to manage the I.T. in his place. I'm not familiar with all the reports as I've been on the job barely a week. Is there a report number or code so I can ask to have it printed for you?"

"It is headed C.A.I.R. and shows the date of the report. I don't think that there is any particular report number," he says.

"With George gone and some of his staff too, I'll have to ask around for it. Is it produced every Friday?"

"Yes. The last one I received is dated December 18th."

"It will take me a few days to find the report and then generate it. I suppose I might as well produce the one for next Friday too. Can you come back next Friday at 2:30. I should be able to have all the reports for you by then? Let me have your number so I can call if I'm unable to have it ready for you," I say.

He agrees, gives me his card and I see him out.

I call Peter Rabin and ask for a list of reports.

"I'm looking for the C.A.I.R. report. It's supposed to be generated every Friday for a research project," I say. "I need the report for each week after December 18th. If you find it, please print the last six reports for me."

Half an hour later, Peter is in my office with the reports for December and January.

"What do they show?" I ask. "Is it some kind of statistics?"

"Not really," Peter tells me. "It's more a chart showing the time that something occurs each day for the week for a list of codes. I think the codes identify the building and apartment being monitored. That's the first part and it has one chart for each apartment. The second part is a list of words with a number after each word. I think the number is the number of times the word is used. The word list is quite short."

"Does it report on every apartment?" I ask.

"Oh no. It's only about twenty apartments and although some are the same, each week the list is slightly different," he says. "The ones after December 18th are all for the same apartments as those on Dec 18th, so I would think that Kirkman changes the parameters for each report."

I think about it for a while and ask Peter for any lists he has found of code tables showing what codes mean and a list of each report he gets.

"Do the operating manuals have a sample of each report?" I ask.

"Yes, everything is fairly well documented."

"Tomorrow, if you can find the time, please get me all the sample report documentation and all the code lists you can find," I request.

"It's impossible," he says. "The manuals take up a whole wall of shelves from floor to ceiling in the operations room. You will have to go there to look at them."

I accept his view and say that I'd be there tomorrow at 10. I ask him to be ready to explain as much of it as he can at that time.

"I'm concentrating on the A.I. part," I say.

"It's all A.I." he replies.

Tuesday at 10 I start a review of the sorts of reports that the A.I. system is generating. It turns out that the reports for Dunphy are intermediate data. Many of the reports for Parker subsidiaries are in the form of conclusions. For example, the renting office gets a list of apartments that might become available over the next three months with a percentage indicating how likely it is that the apartment will be available. The moving business gets a list of people likely to want the services of a moving company. The grocery businesses that are supplying the onsite stores get extremely specific lists of items to be delivered to each apartment building.

I wonder if similarly, complete reports are available to Dunphy. We can't find any.

I ask Peter to see if Parker is sending data files anywhere and he points out that all they need to do is send a link and a password and any authorized person can access the raw data in the cloud.

By the time my coffee break arrives, I am so full of information I am confused. I go to Starbucks, but Kate doesn't show.

She isn't there on Wednesday either. On Thursday she does arrive, and I made the point of asking her to be sure to be at Starbucks at 3 p.m. Friday.

"It will be interesting for you," I suggest.

I take some copies of reports to my apartment to study at night. I feel I have enough to use to catch Dunphy off guard. I plan to surprise him with Kate and watch how the two of them react.

Dunphy arrives at 2:30 on Friday, and we sit down in my office while I hand him the reports he is missing and ask if these are the ones he wants. He says that they are and asks me if I could send electronic copies in the future. I promise to attach report files to emails. I don't query the lack of security with such a scheme, just go along with it.

I invite him to join me for a coffee at Starbucks and we stroll over, arriving at five minutes after three. After we order, I pay. We pick up the aromatic coffee, and approach the table where Kate is sitting with her back to us. I remove my mask and Rob does likewise. I pull out a chair opposite Kate for Rob, asking "May we join you?" and I take another. Kate looks up and exclaims "Ted Simmons! Where the hell did you come from? I thought you were dead!"

I am watching Rob closely and I must admit that he plays it rather well.

"Hi Kate," he says. "Not dead yet!"

Then he turns to me and asks, rather pointedly, if I've set him up. I say that he owes me, considering the nonsense he's been selling about C.A.I.R.

"You work for C.S.I.S., not C.A.I.R.," I say. "What is C.S.I.S. doing with those Parker reports? I think that we're being used. How does the C.A.I.R. report fit into all this?" I ask.

He tries to change the subject by asking Kate how she is doing. He knows that she is getting well-paid to keep out of the way.

"What are you doing consorting with this Parker man, Kate? You are supposed to stay away. That's why we're paying you."

"Don't mind him, Kate," I say.

I give Dunphy a serious look.

"If I don't get a straight answer, I'm going to blow this scheme sky high," I threaten.

"No coffee for you today, Jenkins," Dunphy states. "You are under arrest," he says as he pulls out his cell and makes a quick call.

"Forget it," I say. "C.S.I.S. doesn't have police powers. You can't arrest me. This is more bull."

"You are both under arrest," say Dunphy. "Kate, you are under arrest for spying on behalf of a foreign power; and you, Jenkins, are under arrest for attempting to blackmail a public servant."

"You can't arrest anyone," I say.

"Maybe not," agrees Dunphy, "but perhaps Sergeant Edwards can."

He looks up over my shoulder and I turn to see a large R.C.M.P. officer in a navy-blue trench coat walking towards us.

"Let's go quietly," Edwards suggests. "We wouldn't want to make a fuss, would we?"

Kate and I stand. I cover my amazement and chagrin with my handy mask. There is an R.C.M.P. station wagon parked illegally on Wellington. I decide not to point out that infraction. Kate and I are hustled into the back seat and the door slams shut. I notice there are no inside handles to open the doors. A plastic partition separates us from the front. Dunphy and Edwards get in and begin silently discussing their next move.

I turn to Kate.

"What's new with you?" I ask.

Chapter 16

The drive to Ottawa takes the usual couple of hours. With the traffic in Ottawa, it is close to six when we stop in front of the Elgin Street Police Station. We are escorted into the station and placed in different rooms, so we can't compare ideas and come up with a consistent story to rationalize our crimes. Mind you, we spent the last two hours chatting in the back of the station wagon.

On the ride, I ask Kate about the "spying for a foreign country" that Dunphy mentioned.

"Is that Zimbabwe or South Africa?" I ask her.

"Oh, it could be either," she says. "In South Africa, the department is called State Security Agency. They handle foreign intelligence gathering as well as counter-intelligence work. That's much like Canada's C.S.I.S. In Zimbabwe, the agency is called the Central Intelligence Organisation, but they concentrate on political rivals rather than foreign spies."

I notice that she hasn't answered my question. It sounds more like a prepared diversionary tactic.

"I think you said that you were born in Zimbabwe and moved to South Africa in 2016. Is that right?"

"That's my story and I'm sticking to it," she says as she laughs. "When you are accused of anything, don't keep changing your story. How are you going to handle the charge of attempted blackmail?"

"I have no idea," I say. "Maybe I'll just keep my big mouth shut for once."

"In any case, old man, we may not meet again, so I want to say 'Thank you' for accepting me as a damsel in distress that Sunday night in the Bayshore Inn. You did try to help, I admit," she tells me.

"Just to satisfy my curiosity, who picked you up and stole my car on the peninsula road?" I ask.

"Can't say, I'm afraid. I will admit I phoned for backup. You'll have to live with not knowing who came. Will that spoil your "Case of" story?"

"Not really. It's all fiction. I'll make up something believable," I say. "You expect that you'll be deported, I presume. You might as well look on the bright side; you'll be reunited with your daughter."

"I expect you are right about being deported. If you promise to keep this between us, she isn't my daughter. Her Mom was killed in a car accident and I'm using her Mom's identity. The daughter is living with her aunt."

"Don't say anything in the car that you don't want the police to know. They may be recording it," I caution.

"It doesn't matter. I'm getting tired of this cold weather. South Africa is warm and sunny at this time of year. I'll be happy to be back."

We sit in silence for the rest of the ride.

After I'm sitting alone in the police station for an hour, Dunphy and a uniformed Ottawa police officer enter the room. Dunphy says that I'm not under arrest, merely detained for questioning. As they do not consider me to be a flight risk, they say I can go, provided I promise to show up for a meeting with C.S.I.S. brass at headquarters tomorrow morning.

They give me the address for the meeting and call a taxi for me.

I eat supper in my hotel room while trying to decide my next steps. At 8 o'clock I call Charlie to touch base.

"Hi, Bill. Congratulations! You've survived two weeks and Parker hasn't report a problem. That's great."

"Well, it's been quite an education for me," I say. "The credit should go to Allen, Rabin and Steubins. They are terrific. How is your new update working out? Many bugs?"

"It's keeping me busy, although no worse than the previous one," he says.

"I wondered if you've have heard any complaints from Parker. There's no word there about Kirkman's condition or when he'll be back. I don't suppose you've heard anything, have you?"

"No. I'm sure you will hear before I do," he says.

"Okay. If there's nothing else, I'll say have a good weekend, then."

"Right. Goodnight."

We disconnect and I heave a sigh.

'I'm a coward,' I say to myself. 'How will I tell him I'm detained in Ottawa, accused of blackmailing a public servant, and about to be interrogated by C.S.I.S.?'.

I go to bed after setting an alarm on my phone and, as well, asking for a wake-up call in the morning. I don't want to miss my morning meeting.

I take a taxi to the Ogilvie Road address, arriving with ten minutes to spare. I wait in the lobby where Rob Dunphy finds me just before the scheduled meeting. We take an elevator to the top floor and go into a spacious conference room.

Dunphy introduces me to Assistant Director Murray who waves 'Hello' and in turn introduces me to the man standing beside him.

"I don't believe you've met George Kirkman," he says. "George, this is William Jenkins. He's been covering for you at Parker."

I bump elbows with the I.T. professional whose systems I have been managing for a couple of weeks.

"It's nice to meet you at last, Mr. Kirkman," I say.

"I appreciate that you and your team helped immensely during my covid-19 illness," he says. "I'm pretty well over it and should be back at work in a week or two."

I am careful to be a good six feet away from Kirkman as we sit down for our meeting.

Murray starts it out.

"Rob thinks it is time to bring you into the picture in more detail. However, we did find some things that bother me, and I'd like to clear them up. Our records show a William Jenkins, born in 1932, with a secret security clearance obtained in 1960. Do you have a security clearance, Mr. Jenkins?"

"That is probably my father. He died in 1970. No, I haven't required a clearance in any of my work," I say.

"What we're about to discuss requires top secret clearance and there isn't time to go through all the formalities. Would you be willing to accept the conditions of a clearance based on your swearing allegiance to the Crown?" he asks.

"Certainly," I say.

He has me raise my right hand, place my left on the Bible and swear to uphold something or other. All I have to say is "I do" at the end of his speech. 'No worse than getting married' I think.

We turn to the matter at hand. I decide to follow my own advice and don't volunteer a word.

"We know, Mr. Jenkins, that you have discovered that we are using Parker to gather intelligence for the security of Canada. Your study of all the reports, as we learned from one of the computer operators, leads us to that conclusion. Is that correct?"

"Yes," I admit.

"What you don't know is that our friend George Kirkman is originally Giorgi Kastikoff from Russia."

"Actually, I do know that" I say, breaking my rule about shutting up.

"What? How did you know that?" he asks.

"Kate told me when she described the CBC contract investigation that she and Ted Simmons are doing. Ted missed a meeting that they planned to have with George."

Rob broke in with an explanation.

"Remember, sir, you called me back to Ottawa on that Saturday night."

"You mean to tell me, Jenkins, that you've been working with this Kate Ngobani since then?" Murray asks.

"Not really working with her, but, yes, that information led me to seek more information. I wonder if George here, is Russian Mafia or a sleeper agent. If I discover that he is, I plan to blow the whistle."

Murray looks at Kirkman and nods.

"He was an agent originally. The Americans caught on, turned him, and are using him to send fake information to the Russians. When the pandemic came, they asked us to maintain control."

He turns to Rob.

"Dunphy, why in heaven's name did you bring this South African woman into the picture?" he asks.

"We know she is an agent," Rob explained. "We are watching her. She is here to gather some sort of information, but we can't find out what her mission is. We gave her something to do where we can control her."

"So," I summarize, "the South African spy and the Canadian counter spy, with the help of the Russian spy, keep track of the foreign spies who happen to rent apartments from Parker. Is that what this is all about?" I ask.

Dunphy volunteers to answer.

"I wouldn't put it in those stark terms, but essentially, yes, we are recording all conversations in specific Ottawa apartments rented to diplomats and their employees. Parker has the A.I. capability to analyze conversations. They use tenants' conversations to decide what services to offer to their tenants."

"I wonder about the privacy clause in that lease agreement," I say. "I suppose that's what makes spying on Canadians legal, eh?"

Murray jumps in to make sure we understand that they are working on diplomats, not Canadian citizens.

"Everything is fair in spying and counter-intelligence," he says. "We don't spy on the apartments where Canadians live. We specify which ones Kirkman is to use."

Trying to throw a little dust in their eyes, I ask as innocently as possible, about their control of Kirkman.

"How do you know that good old Giorgi isn't still sending reports to Russia or America or other countries such as, for example, China. The Parker system sends files into the IBM cloud and with proper identification and passwords, anyone with access to the cloud can get any report held there. How closely are you monitoring George? Incidentally, George, what did you do wrong to get the CIA on your tail originally?" I ask.

Of course, I have no idea whether the cloud data can be shared, but it seems a good idea to turn the focus onto George rather than yours truly.

Before they can respond to those questions, I add another issue.

"Is George really suffering from covid-19 or is that just a cover so he can get some more time with your people?" I ask.

"How much of this activity do you share with Parker management? My impression is that they are incredibly good at what they do, but don't have any interest in or knowledge of what the I.T. department is doing. Who is in on this intelligence project?" I ask.

By this time, I am beginning to feel that I am running the meeting. I try to end it all by saying that I hope that they can get George back on the job no later than the end of the week or else I might have to go up the chain of command to make things happen. That is possibly a step too far.

Murray says: "Let me remind you, Jenkins, that you are bound by the Official Secrets Act. What we discuss today is top secret. You must not mention it to your fellow IBM staff members or with the people at Parker. Dunphy will be your handler until Kirkman is back. We'll try to make it next Friday, but we have a lot to cover with him.

As far as going up the chain of command is concerned, I can assure you that not only is the Commissioner of the R.C.M.P. fully aware of this project, but also the cabinet members with oversight of C.S.I.S. activities are up to speed on it. Don't make waves. Don't even suggest making waves."

I rise to my feet and say, "Okay, I've got the picture. I want to be out of Parker as soon as possible. If you can be back by a week Monday, George, I'd appreciate it."

I thank everyone as though it was my meeting. Dunphy leaps to his feet.

"I'll see you out, Bill."

We walk to the elevator, get to the reception area and I order a cab. Rob waits silently with me and wishes me well as I head to the taxi.

'That went well,' I think. 'At least I'm not in jail.'

The taxi takes me to the train station. I catch the 3:30 Via to Linden.

The whole next week I pretend that I am managing I.T. at Parker whereas I am simply finishing writing this story.

By January 25th I have 'The Case of the Intrepid Investigator' ready for printing. I submit it to Amazon and on February 16th my proof copy arrives.

I am clear about these dates because this is Edition 2. Edition 1 ends a couple of paragraphs above. It comes out as a best seller, sort of. Seventeen copies are printed. Fifteen are author copies for friends and family; one sale is made to C.S.I.S. and another to the R.C.M.P.

This is the page where I should admit that I am the Intrepid Investigator. I left the relevant paragraph on page 19 as is, just to keep you, my readers, in suspense.

Postscript

It turns out that C.S.I.S., the R.C.M.P. and the Canadian Justice system are all staffed by people who lack a sense of humour. I spell out very clearly that this is a work of fiction. Any resemblance with any person living or dead is purely coincidental. These organizations and their staff members take themselves much too seriously. They see crimes everywhere they look.

I learned a great deal because of this project. I'm a little more familiar with IBM, big data, A.I. and neural networks.

I'm also now much more familiar with the Canadian criminal justice system.

It turns out that a trial 'in camera' means one in which there are no cameras. That's typical governmental doublespeak. As well, there are no reporters, no journalists, and no public spectators. Only government witnesses who bend the facts to meet their needs can witness the trial.

Trials 'in camera' are quick.

The prosecutor says: "He published it!" (Dunphy testifies that I published details of a counter-spy investigation and my revelations threaten the security of the Western World.)

My defense lawyer says: "It is fiction!" and points out my disclaimer.

The judge notes that I have violated the Official Secrets Act because I have written and published the details of what has happened in a C.S.I.S. investigation and that it is dangerous and illegal to reveal the counter-espionage methods of the Government of Canada.

He concludes: "Guilty as charged. Eighteen years for you, Jenkins!"

He does chastise C.S.I.S. for actions which, if improperly described as in what he calls 'this fictitious novel', might give the appearance that C.S.I.S. staff are spying on Canadians, which would be outside their mandate.

The court exonerates Parker and praises them as forward-looking for using A.I. to be more competitive. They donate another million to a charity working with homeless youth and replace Kirkman with a pleased Ms. Barbara Allen, whose income more than doubles.

Kate returns to South Africa on a military aircraft that winds its way to Cape Town.

Kirkman turns out to be a triple spy working for Russia, USA, and Canada. He is trying to sell his A.I. system to South Africa, China, and France. He is told not to do that and given consulting and teaching roles within C.S.I.S.

The court exonerates Tom Scully. His statement about knowing nothing of the plot stands him in good stead.

The R.C.M.P. don't bother to find out who Harry and Alec are because their role is not central to the crime.

The court decides that Charlie and IBM are unknowingly involved. C.S.I.S. doesn't tell anyone that George Kirkman is under their control and when the I.T. management team is struck down by covid, C.S.I.S. lets Parker solve their staffing problem by calling on IBM. However, the court does issue a statement warning IBM and other companies that they must ensure that their A.I. applications are not used for illegal purposes.

It turns out that I get to choose which minimum-security prison I wish to attend to serve my sentence. I choose William Head at Metchosen, BC about 25 km southwest of Victoria on the southern-most tip of Vancouver Island because the climate there is mild, and I enjoy the view of the ocean.

My usual duties are related to landscaping and care of the greens on the prison's golf course. My handicap is coming down and eventually, I suppose, I'll be able to shoot my age. I've been scoring about 100 on a good day. With good behaviour, I'll be out of here in 2027 so if I can get my score down to 95 by then, this will have been worth it.

One advantage of living with my fellow inmates is that I hear many stories that I will use to take my "Case of" series to the end of the alphabet.

Sadly, of course, a criminal cannot profit from his crimes, so I will donate all the profit generated by sales of this Second Edition of a 'true crime fiction', namely 'The Case of the Intrepid Investigator' to my favourite charity.

(If you believe that, maybe you should look for a copy of "The Case of the Jenkins Jailbird" on sale in bookstores everywhere.)

Here are the pages of 'The Case of the Jenkins Jailbird', the next amazing story of the adventures of author and adventurer William (Bill) Jenkins.

The Case of the Jenkins Jailbird

Edition 1

Published by William Jenkins

Email: williamhenryjenkins@gmail.com

Telephone: 1-613-217-0940

The Case of the Jenkins Jailbird

For my many inmate friends,

Who celebrated the closing of K.P.

and the opening of Millhaven

1971

The Case of the Jenkins Jailbird

Chapter 1

Because I can choose which minimum-security prison that I wish to attend to serve my 18-year sentence for violating the Official Secrets Act, I pick William Head at Metchosen, BC about 25 km southwest of Victoria on the southern-most tip of Vancouver Island. The climate there is mild, and I enjoy the view of the ocean.

I am escorted there by a staff member of Corrections Canada, a bright, cheerful graduate of the Canadian Corrections course at the Linden Community College, Peter Dagenais.

"You're lucky," Peter tells me. "Starting next week, they'll be outsourcing the escort function. You'll probably be handcuffed and handled by someone who hasn't had the proper course. If I were you, I'd avoid requesting going anywhere away from William Head. Give them some time to learn how to escort properly."

"I'm not likely to be going anywhere," I reply. "I'll be here for six years before I'm eligible to apply for parole. I don't suppose they will let me scoot off to Victoria for afternoon tea at the Empress Hotel."

"You never know. Once you get settled, the other inmates will clue you in on how to play the system."

Peter is driving the station wagon on the last leg of my journey from Ottawa. It's only about 40 km from the Victoria International airport to the prison at Metchosin and we're getting close. I'm in the passenger seat, not handcuffed or restrained in any way other than by the usual seat belt. Peter says, when I am placed in his custody at the airport in Ottawa, that I'm not a flight risk, so we might as well enjoy the trip.

I can see the ocean in the distance and to a certain extent, I'm looking forward to a little fresh air after many days in Ottawa awaiting my trial. I admit that once the trial gets going, the court part doesn't take too long. 'Slam, bam, in the can,' I remember.

The car rolls up to the gate. Peter hands the guard a slip of paper and the gate opens. We approach a largish cottage and Peter parks in a visitor slot. We walk in, me with my suitcase of allowable possessions, Peter following behind. I'm greeted by a receptionist who asks: "Mr. Jenkins?" Clearly, I'm expected.

I won't go into all the details, but these are civilised people and I'm treated well.

Peter says 'Goodbye' and I thank him for the ride and the company as he heads back to Victoria. I'm settled into my room, given a special uniform, and then led to the mess hall for lunch. So far, it's as though I'm back in the Air Force, except instead of living in barracks with 20 others, I'm sharing a room with one other guy in a townhouse.

After lunch I get the mandatory visit with and lecture from Joseph P. McCarthy, Warden of this "Club Fed" institution. He welcomes me, goes over a few minor details mostly related to security. To my surprise, he says "I don't think you'll be here very long, Bill."

I'm not sure if he means I'll be dead before the day is out or if the government is closing the place.

He goes on to explain that he's received a message from Ottawa saying that my conviction and sentence are being appealed. I know that my lawyer, George Harrison, made some comment about that after the trial, but I certainly don't expect anything to happen quickly, knowing how slowly the wheels of justice usually turn. 'Maybe,' I think, 'they will do an appeal in camera. If that works as quickly as a trial in camera, it won't take long.'

"By the way," he says, after I call him Mr. McCarthy a couple of times, "we're informal here. You can call me 'Joe'. Everyone will know who you mean."

His welcome and the place in general are quite encouraging.

I'm authorized to use my laptop any time for writing. It's just that using the Internet requires supervision and is done on their computers in a computer room set up with a dozen PC's.

After my discussion with the warden, I meet my roommate, Tom Voight, and he tells me the do's and don'ts. Tom has been here for three years now and expects to get out next July. His job is a clerical one, delivering mail in the morning, but he gets every afternoon off and spends his time either reading or playing golf. He warns me not to ask any inmate about what they did to get here.

"You simply don't ever bring up the subject. Some inmates are especially sensitive about it," he says.

It seems I'll be working in the library, which makes sense to me. I've certainly been in enough libraries over the years.

To my surprise, only a week into my incarceration here, I'm called in to see the warden.

"Good news, Bill," he says, "you can pack your bags for a trip to Ottawa. It seems that your lawyer has arranged for an immediate in camera review of your case. You're out of here tomorrow."

"That's crazy," I reply. "Why here and back in such a short time?"

"The rumour I hear is that the Association of Mystery Writers of Canada got to the Prime Minister and are threatening to leak the details of your trial to the press. He doesn't want another scandal so this may be 'Goodbye'. Good luck, old man."

Rather dazed by the sudden change, I return to my room and pack up. I gather I'll be picked up at 7 a.m.

The new escort service is on time. As Peter predicted, I'm handcuffed and stuck in the back seat of a car. The driver introduces herself as Vicky Rogers but says little else. On the exterior of the car is an identifying sign

'High Society Escorts'. I sit quietly for the ride to Victoria airport.

Vicky is a rather striking young lady wearing a khaki uniform and matching khaki cap. As we approach the airport, she peels off the highway, taking the route to the area for private aircraft. She parks beside a hangar and says she'll be a couple of minutes. Ten minutes later she returns with a couple of men dressed in similar khaki duds.

They haul me out of the car and march me to the front of the hangar where a twin-engine Aerostar is sitting with its cabin door open. The interior of the aircraft is modified to have only two passenger seats. The rear of the cabin is behind a door and, of course, the pilot area is also closed off. One man, the pilot I assume, heads to the cockpit, while the other stays outside and stands in view of the captain, making sure all is clear.

Vicky and I sit in the chairs.

"Can you take off the handcuffs?" I ask.

"Not just yet," she replies. "We're waiting for Hank to get in."

The propellers turn over and catch. Hank arrives a minute or two later, pulls up the steps and closes the door.

"Okay, we can go to the cell now," Vicky says.

She leads me to the back part of the aircraft, closes and locks the door behind me. It's pitch dark, no windows, although before she closes the door, I see a chair and I inch towards it. She turns on the lights and says: "Hold still."

Mercifully, she removes my handcuffs and I rub my wrists to try to get the circulation going again. We sit down and buckle up because the aircraft starts taxiing. About ten minutes later we lift off and start the journey towards Ottawa.

An information light turns on indicating that we can unbuckle. Vicky stands up and moves towards me.

"Stand up," she says.

I have no idea as to what she has in mind, but I unbuckle the seat belt and get to my feet.

"Help me with this table," she says.

There's a full-length single-bed-size table against the wall that is covered with a foam mattress. We move it to the centre aisle and Vicky shows me how to set its height. She hands me a towel and I look at her, trying to figure out what is going on.

"Take off your clothes," she says. "It's time for your massage."

"Massage?"

"All part of the High Society Escort service," she informs me.

We had stops in Regina and Thunder Bay for fuel. Vicky and I had lunch and then dinner between massages. By the time I got to Ottawa, I had a smile on my face that I didn't lose for weeks.

Chapter 2

Vicky accompanies me to the Chateau Laurier hotel and tells me I am on my own. After I check in, I phone my lawyer and agree to meet him at the courthouse at 10 a.m. tomorrow.

The hearing is rather perfunctory. It, too, is held in camera.

They claim that the prosecutor had misunderstood the information provided by C.S.I.S. and that, in fact, I haven't violated the Official Secrets Act. The judge apologizes and states that he understands that honest mistakes can be made, especially in areas that do not come up frequently. He vacates my conviction and sentence and tells me I am free to go.

My lawyer asks the judge: "What compensation do you recommend that my client be paid for the damage to his reputation, his time incarcerated and the inconvenience of travelling to British Columbia and back?"

"That will be between your client and C.S.I.S.," the judge states.

We clear the courtroom and Assistant Director Murray beckons me over. I introduce my lawyer, George Harrison, and Murray nods.

"No hard feelings, I hope, Mr. Jenkins," he says. "I have one minor document for you to sign and then this will be all over."

"May I see it, please?" George asks.

George suggests that we all go to a nearby restaurant for a coffee while he reviews what Murray wants me to sign. We find Beckta Fine Dining a block away and choose a table near the back.

We each order coffee while my lawyer digests the two pages.

"I'm sorry, Mr. Murray," he says. "This isn't even close. You're asking us to totally forgive and forget with no compensation. Mr. Jenkins deserves at least $100,000 in damages for what you have done."

'Well, the Director thought I should give it a try. Frankly, I was very much impressed with how well you handled yourself in that meeting we held at headquarters, Bill. I think your talents are being wasted as an author, even though you do write compelling literature."

I guess I'm as susceptible to flattery as anyone else and I asked Murray what he had in mind as my lawyer quietly kicked me under the table.

"We think you could be a great help to our service," he says. "We realise that you are too old to be an employee, but we wondered if you would work with us on a retainer basis. We're thinking of $10,000 a month, guaranteed for at least a year."

"If you throw in the legal fees I have incurred for this false arrest, trial and hearing, I'd certainly be interested," I said.

"Done," said Murray. "I'll draw up the papers and you can come over at 10 tomorrow morning. Bring along Mr. Harrison so we can get a decision right away."

After this short meeting, George and I head to his office, and he runs off his invoice for services rendered.

"I've added two hours for tomorrow's meeting. That will cover your total legal expenses for this. I think you've done well, considering that you could have spent years in B.C. and you're coming out of it with a firm contract for at least a year," he comments.

"It certainly could be worse. I want to chat with the President of the Association of Mystery Writers of Canada and thank him for his support. Without his connection to the PMO, I'd still be cooling my heels at Metchosen. Do you know how to reach him?'

"Actually, the President is a lady, Elizabeth Hamilton. I have her number. She lives in Windsor, but the ones who helped you are here in the Ottawa office. I suggest you talk with them."

"Do you know who has the connection with the PMO? That would be the first one to thank."

"The document I read named Robert Ainslie. Here's his number," George says.

I call but get voice mail. I leave a message thanking him and the Association profusely for their support.

I thank George for all his good work and take a taxi back to the Chateau Laurier. There's just the meeting with Assistant Director Murray tomorrow and then I'll be able to return to Kingston. I enjoy a quiet dinner, reflecting on the strange twists and turns that had brought me to the possibility of getting a lucrative C.S.I.S. contract. 'It was lucky that I have kept the apartment,' I think.

The next morning, George and I show up at C.S.I.S. headquarters and review the proposed contract.

"This doesn't specify what particular work Bill will be doing, simply that he will report to you," George points out. "Can you be more specific about what the work will entail?"

"It's difficult to put that sort of detail into the contract," says Murray. "You aren't trained in much of the sort of work we do, Bill. I expect your first assignment will be to work with one of our counter-intelligence men to understand how we go about a typical investigation."

"Will I be based in Kingston?" I ask.

"Not likely," says Murray. "There is little C.S.I.S. work there. You would work out of Ottawa Headquarters, this building, and be deployed wherever a specific assignment takes you. That's the way most of our staff work. When we are in another city, we work out of the local R.C.M.P. office unless we are doing something clandestine."

"Clandestine?" I query. "Am I likely to be working at that level? I had the impression you were interested in my management skills. Does C.S.I.S. expect me to go undercover?"

"We actually use specialists for undercover work, so you aren't likely to get involved in that. I was thinking that with your computer background, you might contribute to our counter-hacking team. You probably know that many countries have government-backed teams that are acting as cyber criminals, trying to steal corporate secrets and even hacking into government files."

"I certainly heard about the Russians hacking into the U.S. Treasury department, but I didn't expect to hear that they are hacking us. I'm surprised that they think that we are worth bothering about."

"We're a member of the Five Eyes countries, sharing intelligence with the U.S., U.K., Australia, and New Zealand. We are just as likely to be attacked as the U.S., maybe even more so because our security systems are not as advanced as those in the U.K. or the U.S.A. Would work in that area interest you?" Murray asks.

"Certainly," I say. "I've read about ethical hacking and how difficult it is to protect any system connected to the Internet."

Mr. Murray turned to George.

"Mr. Harrison, I'm sure you can understand that the possible assignments can range over a wide variety of topics. I'd rather not limit Bill's duties by explicit wording in the contract. Is there anything else that you would like changed in the agreement?"

"I understand," says George. "Any questions, Bill?"

"What about living expenses," I ask. "I'm currently paying for an apartment in Kingston, and I'd like to return to it when my contract ends. Will you cover my costs when I'm here or on assignment in another place?"

"No problem," says Murray. "You just submit monthly expense reports. Mind you, we won't cover staying at the Chateau Laurier. You could expense the rent of a furnished apartment in Ottawa and hotel expenses anywhere else."

I agree to the terms and sign the document.

"By the way," I mention, "this is the second time I've been at an official C.S.I.S. meeting on a Saturday. Am I expected to work on weekends or is this unusual?"

"This is a 24/7 job, Jenkins." says Murray with a smile. "You are on duty all the time."

"Just like the Air Force," I say, noting that the friendly 'Bill' has been replaced by the more formal 'Jenkins'. "Hurry up and wait," I say, the motto of the military.

"Report here Monday at zero eight hundred hours Monday, Bill," says Murray and we are out the door.

Chapter 3

I remain in the Chateau Laurier for the weekend. I figure there's no point in getting an apartment in Ottawa until I know that I'll be here for some time.

When I arrive at C.S.I.S. Headquarters on Monday, Murray sits down with me and apologizes for our meeting on Saturday.

"Sorry to have wandered off into hacking on Saturday. I don't think your lawyer has much of an idea of our mission," he says.

"Oh, that's alright," I say, not knowing why hacking isn't part of the mission.

"As you know," he continues, "our mission has to do with intelligence on threats to our national security. The Canadian Communications Security Establishment, just down the road, is the group that listens in to all communications and handles hacking and similar threats. Our job is to determine and eliminate threats of terrorism or sabotage from within or without Canada and we conduct operations both here and abroad."

"Of course," I say, as though I knew that all along.

"So CSE is a 'behind the scenes' agency with hackers and people eavesdropping on conversations. Simply put, C.S.I.S. has spies and spy-catchers. Our job is to find anyone who is threatening to act against our country's interests."

"How do you see me fitting in?" I ask.

"Frankly, Bill, I'm afraid you don't fit in. C.S.I.S. was formed fifty years ago when we were split off from the R.C.M.P. Most of our people have police or military background and take several years of training in spy craft. Most speak several languages. They are convincing actors. Your talent seems to be in management, but I can't see placing you in a position of authority over men and women who have worked their way up through years of dangerous work here and abroad. Frankly, strictly between us, I think it would be best if you just go back to Kingston and write your novels on some topic other than our work. We can absorb the cost of your contract for a year. If something comes up where we can use you, I'll get in touch, but don't hold your breath."

"So, you are paying me to keep quiet and out of the way," I conclude.

"I think that's best," he says. "We certainly don't want any publicity in our line of work. We get in enough trouble with our regular staff who tend to go overboard when they find someone who they think is a terrorist. We don't need another exposé in the form of a tell-all novel."

"Okay," I say. "It's the first time I've had an assignment where I'm to do nothing and not write it up. I agree that I'm not a good actor and I'm lousy at languages. With all this covid around, I'm probably smart to stay in my apartment until the vaccine makes it safe to travel and move around. I don't suppose there's any writing I could do, is there?"

"Not really. I appreciate your accepting this, Bill. Please don't tell your lawyer. He's liable to talk to those mystery writers again and stir the pot."

"There's nothing in Kingston for me to do?" I ask.

"No. We've decided that teaming up with Parker was a mistake. We're better to use our own methods for securing intelligence about foreign embassy spies in Canada."

"Well," I say, "this is a bit disappointing, but I'll get over it. I appreciate that you didn't give me a 'make-work' project."

We end the meeting cordially and I am in a taxi, going back to the Chateau Laurier by 9 o'clock. I check out, take the train to Kingston, get my car out of storage and drive to my favourite parking spot, #4, behind my apartment building.

Everything in the apartment is as I left it on my arrest. The furniture needs dusting, and the refrigerator contents are inedible, but other than that, all is well.

On to the next!